GUARDIANS *of* TIME

Time Machine Emergency Sequel

DAN ARTHUR BUSBY

Guardians of Time
Time Machine Emergency Sequel

Copyright © 2021 by Dan Arthur Busby.

Paperback ISBN: 978-1-63812-107-7
Ebook ISBN: 978-1-63812-108-4

All rights reserved. No part in this book may be produced and transmitted in any form or by any means, electronic, or mechanical, including photocopying, recording, or by any information storage and retrieval system, without permission in writing from the copyright owner.

The views expressed in this work are solely those of the author and do not necessarily reflect the views of the publisher hereby disclaims any responsibility for them.

Published by Pen Culture Solutions   08/12/2021

Pen Culture Solutions
1-888-727-7204 (USA)
1-800-950-458 (Australia)
support@penculturesolutions.com

1

The year was 2030...two years after Dennis Carrigan retired, and Alexander the Great became King of The United American Republics. Alexander had ruled the entire time in peace and prosperity, but new developments were very concerning.

As he stood in his office gazing out the window, a knock at the door broke the silence. Without waiting for a response, someone turned the knob and swung the door open. Quickly stepping into the room was professor Kibble, followed closely by Derek.

As Derek softly closed the door, Alexander motioned to the row of plush chairs. "Gentlemen, have a seat." A tone of distress emanated from his voice. Kibble's brow wrinkled as he sat. "You haven't sounded like this in a couple of years." He barely stopped his hand from twisting at his mustache.

Alexander refused to sit down himself, but just stood in front of them, caressing his chin with one hand. Suddenly, his hand dropped, and he began pacing.

After two laps, he stopped and faced his visitors. "Our former enemies, the Chinese and Russians have developed a weapons shutdown system of their own. They have disabled our defenses in their home countries."

Derek and Kibble exchanged glances before Kibble spoke. "Have they launched an attack yet?" A quick nod came from Alexander. "They are exchanging fire as we speak."

Kibble shook his head. "The most important thing right now is finding a way to keep all of their weapons shut down. If they don't disable all of ours, we'll still have the upper hand."

Alexander nervously pulled his sword in and out. "I'll take care of that. You go get Ed started on taking out their system."

As Kibble and Derek headed for the door, Alexander called them back. "I don't want a blood bath on either side." He clenched his teeth before continuing. "I used to enjoy killing, but I'm not the war monger I once was."

Kibble nodded and half-grinned. "You know we'll do our best and will keep you informed." Within ten minutes, the two government officials/scientists were standing at Ed Worth's apartment door ringing the bell.

The door opened, and Ed raised his eyebrows. "Hmm, must be important." He stepped back and motioned for them to come in. "Go ahead," he continued, "let's sit down for whatever bad news you've got."

"Well," after Kibble was seated, he sounded grim, "your perception is pretty sharp." He paused. "Russia and China have developed their own weapons shutdown systems."

Ed's eyes closed, and his head dropped. Kibble ruthlessly went on. "Ed, there's war raging as we speak. We've got to somehow disable their weapons."

Ed raised his head and supported it with his folded hands. He looked at Kibble. "I don't know if I can do that, Kibble. If they have this technology, we may be in a stalemate."

He leaned back and rested one ankle over the other leg. "Oh, I can try a few things, but I can't see any quick solutions." After a short silence, Kibble wrinkled his brow and slapped the arm of his chair. "Well, we'd better get into the C2 and do some scouting."

The C2 was a modern craft adapted to replace the old Dormac. It could hover like a helicopter, but traveled much faster, and had much better weapons.

,m Ed's resigned look said it all. He slowly stood. "Let me get my briefcase." He then slowly shuffled out of the room.

2

The three men made their way out to Kibble's car, with Ed bringing up the rear carrying his precious computerized briefcase.

Ed was a true scientist, from appearance, to demeanor, to purpose. His head bald on top, with a small hair line at ear level. He had a pair of glasses attached to a chain around his neck. Science was his whole life, and he had a way of conquering every challenge that he accepted.

At the aircraft hangar, they walked slowly toward the C2, still trying to iron out a plan of action. Kibble stood at the aircraft, and faced Ed. "We can call in a dozen F4 fighters at any time, but I'd prefer to get this done remotely by flying as close as possible to our targets without coming under attack."

Ed nodded, appearing distracted, as though he were doing calculations in his head. "Just get me in close, and I'll see if I can throw a wrench into their system." He smiled, as if he were playing some new and challenging game.

With everyone seated in the C2, Derek prepared for departure. He appeared nonchalant as he looked over his shoulder. "I'm going to transport us to the Chinese border instantly, as soon as we get into the air."

Seat belts snapped, and the solar powered engine started. The craft's appearance was oval shaped with two short stubby wings.

Shooting straight up, they reached 200 feet in seconds. Derek glanced at Ed. "Just want to make sure your equipment is ready. We may not have much time when we get there."

Ed signaled with a nod. "Go ahead." With a few pokes on the control panel, Derek was ready for the trip.

Two years of time travel experimentation had molded him into an expert. "Here we go!" He warned, as he reached for a switch on the panel, and flipped it on.

Everything became blurry for a few seconds, but then suddenly a popping sound ripped through the air, and eyesight was crystal clear. Outside the window was the Chinese border.

"This is the main military installation!" He called over his shoulder. "I'll give you as much time as I can."

Ed didn't respond but continued tinkering with his control box. Kibble swiveled around in his chair to watch. Ed flipped switches altered wires. He turned knobs and moved levers up and down. After a few minutes of failure, Ed was getting frustrated. "I should have been able to shut them down by now." He complained, glancing out the window frequently.

Kibble eyed the activity on the ground with a pair of binoculars. He was alarmed to see men climbing into about 20 aircraft just below them. "We need to get out of here!" A sense of urgency sprang from his voice.

"Give me a little more time!" Ed sounded angry and pleading at the same time. He was frantically whipping a screwdriver around, tightening and loosening different screws.

Kibble turned to Derek with a frown. Pointing a finger at the control panel, he shouted, "Get us out of here!"

Derek quickly began punching in coordinates. Ed was abusing the weapons box at high speed.

Kibble stared out the window, twisting his mustache in Ernest. His worst fears were realized when he saw a group of jet fighters headed straight for them. They were almost upon them when Ed thrust a button in the weapons control box. Two of the jet fighters lost power and fell, crashing to the ground. About 18 more sped overhead, disappearing into the clouds.

"Looks like their system has jammed ours." He seemed resigned to failure. Derek didn't hesitate. "We have to go back and warn them. Here we go!" The C2 spun briefly, jumping into time travel that would send them home at about present time. Suddenly they appeared back in north America. The king's building stood in front of them, as they hovered 100 feet above ground.

3

Derek zoomed down to the lawn and powered down. Kibble unbuckled as he spoke. "All of us need to see Alexander together."

Within minutes the three men were on the top story. Kibble knocked as he swung the door open. Alexander was pacing the floor as the men entered. He stopped and faced them, appearing tense and nervous.

"I know what's going on. It's all-out war at the borders of Russia and China. Ground forces and F4s are on their way now."

Kibble bore a chagrined look. "We were unsuccessful at shutting their system down."

Ed jumped in. "They have been disabling most of our weapons." He stepped closer and looked into Alexander's eyes. "Right now, we need to worry about the possibility of nuclear war."

With a solemn face, Alexander asked a question. "How long do you need to develop a counter shutdown of their weapons?" Ed shook his head. "Right now, I have no clue."

Alexander pounded a fist into his open palm. "Get on it right away." As Ed turned to leave, Alexander concluded, "Our survival may depend on it."

He stood like a statue in front of Kibble and Derek, before turning and pacing a few more steps. "You know, I sent two groups of F4s to both borders, and none ever returned."

He turned toward the two men. "It may be time to go back and try to fix this."

After a few seconds of silence, Kibble responded. "How far back?"

"A couple years, when we first started the shutdown system. We need to take over before they get a chance to develop their own."

Kibble was a little taken back. "Do you mean we should occupy China and Russia?" Alexander did not flinch. That's exactly what I mean. Once they have the technology, it's too late to stop them. We must squelch all resistance immediately."

Kibble stroked his mustache with one hand. He caught Alexander's eye. "We need to bring Lex. She's very good at tying loose ends together."

Alexander nodded. "Okay, let's meet at the C2 in an hour."

As Derek and professor Kibble headed for Lex's apartment, they got that same familiar feeling. Things were falling apart, and nuclear war could break out at any time Lex had been living alone for about a year. James had gone on a time travel trip, and not returned. No word had come about what happened, or where he was. Lex had a difficult time adjusting to not knowing his fate, or even when or where he had gone.

The two stood on the porch, as the front door opened a crack. Lex peeked through, and then swung the door all the way open. "Wow, something must be happening for both of you to be here at once."

Derek and Kibble both nodded. "Something is happening." Kibble replied. "So, I see." She smiled. "Why don't you come in?"

The men filed through quickly, faces somber, expressions anxious. "Okay, what is it? I know it's not good." Lex stopped in the living room, turning her palms up.

Kibble did not sit down, but simply engaged eye contact. His hands clutched his hips. "We'll be doing some emergency time traveling." He let this sink in, while Lex's mouth gaped open. "We do have a war going on, which could turn nuclear at any time."

Lex frowned, as she shook her head. She brushed back her red hair and sat down. Pressing her hands together, she faced downward, and said nothing. She then looked up at Kibble. "So how far back are we going?"

Kibble took a seat on the couch. "We'll try a couple of years. They've figured out our weapons shutdown system. Now they've shutdown most of ours."

Derek joined in. "I figure by tomorrow, this country will by occupied. We need to do something about it!"

4

Alexander stood waiting for them at the C2. As the team approached, he motioned for them to gather around him.

They joined him in a circle, and he began to speak. "Before we go, we must discuss our plan. Have you talked about this yet?"

Kibble nodded. "We decided we should go back two years to give us a chance to take over and stop all enemy shutdown research."

Alexander blinked and sort of looked around. Lex burst out with a short laugh, while shrugging her shoulders. "Do you guys realize that we won't be able to talk to our younger selves? It won't be that easy to tell them what we think they should do."

Derek responded. "We'll think of some way to communicate with them. I mean just the fact that the C2 will be there will tell them that something important is happening."

Kibble nodded. "This is important enough that we really don't have a choice. We've got to somehow get across to them that they must bring in the military to initiate marshal law."

"That's right!" Alexander agreed, emphatically pumping his fist. "No more being too nice."

Lex took the initiative again. "I just think you all should realize that it's not gonna be that easy. There will be two of each of us and coming from different perspectives."

She looked from face to face for a moment before speaking. "We can't leave yet. We need Ed Worth."

Kibble's face lit up. "What were we thinking? We'll probably need his expertise with the shutdown system."

Derek pulled out a phone. I'll give him a call and go pick him up." He walked briskly toward the car.

Within a half hour, he came rolling back with Ed in the passenger's seat. They quickly got out and walked toward the C2. Ed was carrying the weapons box.

Alexander briefly spoke to him. "This country will be taken over soon by our enemies. We are going back two years to put things back in our favor."

Ed nodded and smiled. "I'm delighted you remembered me."

Alexander opened the door and beckoned for everyone to board. There were eight comfortable seats available, but five people sat down and buckled in.

Alexander spoke to Derek, who was awaiting instructions. "Just take us above the government building, and hover. Then we'll go back two years."

Derek started the quiet, prop-less craft, slowly lifting straight up. He buzzed over to the capitol building. The trip was short, and he glided to about 20 feet over the top floor.

He punched in some data and looked at his passengers. "Everyone ready?" His eyes met four faces that bore unconvinced looks, as though they weren't sure about the success of this mission. Kibble and Alexander both nodded, so Derek flipped the switch.

5

The horizon popped into view suddenly, as the C2 hovered gently above the capitol building. "Okay, slowly glide down to the front lawn." Alexander wasted no time dispensing orders. "We'll just make an appearance and see what happens."

Derek bit his lip nervously, while he eased the craft sideways and downward.

"You do remember last time we tried this." Lex showed off her recently acquired assertiveness skills. "We could hardly see or hear our counterparts. Communication might just be impossible."

"All is not lost." Kibble chipped in. "We can talk to someone else, who can relay the message."

The C2 approached the ground, as the wheels lowered, and softly touched on the grass. Passersby stared at the unfamiliar aircraft. Security came out immediately, weapons in hand. Ten men steadily approached, talking on radio, and appearing very cautious.

"Out of the aircraft!" The leader barked. Everyone in the C2 exchanged glances and began to step out. "Hands up!" The order rang out. Everyone complied.

When they got close enough, Alexander posed a question. "Do you not recognize me? I am Alexander, the emperor." The leader acted as though he were going to strike Alexander with the butt of his rifle but decided against it. "Straight ahead! Follow those men!"

The time travelers marched with befuddled expressions on their faces. Into the building they went, being led into a stairwell, and down to the basement. A security man opened a door, motioning for them to file in. The door was locked again, and guards were posted outside.

All was quiet, as the five travelers stared at one another in disbelief. "Seems that we caught an alternate time thread." Derek broke the silence.

Lex sighed, placing hands on hips. "Well, this is obviously not Alexander's kingdom. It's more like a police state."

Alexander suddenly turned his head. "This is our best chance to escape! Right away, before they get more security involved."

He started for a window, which was just above his head. Pulling up a chair, he stepped onto the seat, and gazed back at his fellow prisoners. "Stay here. I will be right back." He paused. "Stand on that side of the room, close to the door. Derek, follow me!"

Derek snapped into motion, as Alexander pulled a latch, opening the window, which was about 1x2 feet. He jumped, and Derek helped boost him through. Then Derek jumped while Kibble boosted him through. Outside, the two men looked around.

Alexander quickly started off toward the corner of the building, knowing the C2 was just around the corner. Peering around the edge, he noted that three men guarded their craft.

Glancing back at Derek, he nodded the go signal. He then shoved off, breaking into a soft run. Derek, though petrified, kept pace with him.

The three security men were busy rummaging through the inside of the C2 and did not see them coming.

Alexander broke into a dead run, and got to one who had the door open, and was leaning over, looking inside. He was dispatched by a door slam, followed by a fist to the forehead.

The two remaining guards started bringing up their rifles, but Alexander leaped inside the craft, flipping over in midair, and landing on his back. Kicking with both feet, he delivered a blow to each of their heads, knocking them out cold. Derek stood gazing, showing uncontrolled jaw dropping.

"Help me get him out!" Alexander implored. Derek snapped to it, grabbing one guard, then the other, and scooting them to the ground.

"Okay, get in!" Alexander shouted while he jumped into the co-pilot seat.

6

"I know what to do!" Derek announced, while staring at the screen. He pecked away on the keyboard, occasionally glancing at the building. Slapping the last key with gusto, he looked up in expectation. The transport mechanism kicked in, doing its thing. Soon a boom rang out.

The two men blinked at the inside of the room they had just escaped from. Kibble, Lex, and Ed, recovering from initial shock, ran for the C2, and jumped in.

The two guards outside the door scrambled to unlock it. Meanwhile, Derek raced to program something…anything to get out of there. The guards finally unlocked the door as the sequence was starting. They raised their rifles, and two shots rang out.

The copilot window had been rolled down, and Alexander held a rifle with a smoking barrel. The guards had dropped to the floor, each with a leg wound.

The C2 finished cycling out and burst through to somewhere. All suddenly was quiet, as five heads turned to see sand dunes, drifting like a great sea. The wind blew sand against the windows, suggesting a deserted wasteland.

Lex gasped. "Look behind us! Get us out of here!" Everyone turned and scarcely could believe what they saw. A giant crab-like creature approached, appearing to be about 15 feet tall.

Derek focused on the screen. "One hundred fifty million years ago?! Holy…" His fingers whizzed along, programming ahead 149 million years.

Once again, the cycle started, completing just as the monster banged against the outer shell. The aircraft was abruptly thrust onto the edge of a sandy beach. At the edge of the beach was a world of plush grass, three feet tall.

"Let's stop here for a few minutes." Alexander's voice rang out. He opened his door and stepped out. A gush of sweet, warm air greeted his nostrils. Taking a deep breath, he held it for just a moment. "Wow!" He couldn't help commenting. "Everyone let's get out and have a discussion. I've never breathed such fresh air."

Doors opened, and travelers stepped onto the clean white sand. Gazing across the tall grass, they saw a herd of something fairly close by. "Hey, that's buffalo!" Derek exclaimed. "This is one million years before our time!"

The group gravitated into a circle and sat cross legged in the sand. Alexander shook his head. "Our mission escapes us. We need to get back on track somehow."

Kibble looked up and into each pair of eyes. "At this point, I don't know how to successfully reach two years before our time."

Lex sat up straight, reflecting an air of confidence. "Derek, did you make a mistake trying to send us back two years?" Derek did not flinch or blink. "I was sure the coordinates were correct. I don't know what happened."

Lex eyed Derek, flipping her hair back with one toss of her head. "I know what happened, and I'm not even a scientist."

The group sat in silence, waiting for an explanation. Lex drew a line in the sand with a stick. "The laws of physics, or whatever, wouldn't let us get close to our counterparts. Sure, it sort-of happened before, I don't know how. But this time...no!"

Ed nodded with conviction. "Yes, I can understand why you cannot come face to face with your earlier or later self."

"Or even in the same vicinity." Kibble added. "We got close to our counterparts before, but we couldn't see or hear them legibly."

Alexander raised both hands. "We now realize that we can't go directly back and talk with ourselves. At this point, we must take a different approach."

Kibble twisted his mustache nervously. "Are we desperate enough to try and change history again?" Heads began nodding around the circle.

7

Kibble took the lead once again, posing a question. "We need suggestions as to a time and place in history to make changes that would benefit us."

He could see the wheels turning all around the circle. The silence continued until Derek began to speak. "I don't know a lot about history, but it seems to me that we could have more of an influence on China if we went during the 1800s."

Ed smiled. "Sure, visiting before modern weapons would make it easier. But does anyone here speak Chinese?"

"Ah, no." Kibble conceded. "But I think a better time would be between 1948 to 1949. This was an important time in the history of China. In 1949, Mao Zedong's communists defeated Chiang Kai-shek, who was trying to develop a democracy. Had he been successful, history would have been much different."

Alexander's eyebrows raised. "That does sound like a key time to interfere. We could make big changes if we pushed the right buttons."

Lex suddenly raised her head to speak. "I didn't learn much history either. But by chance, I remembered something. Chiang...whatever...had a wife that spoke perfect English."

Kibble nodded approvingly and began to get excited. "If she spoke English so well, there's a chance that the president himself knew some English.

Derek expanded on the subject. "The weapons on the C2 are very formidable for the 1940s, but our trump card is going to be the weapons shutdown system. Think of scanning the communists and rendering them helpless!"

"Exactly!" Ed added exuberantly. "We would need satellites for nukes, but the Chinese didn't have nukes then." He looked around the circle. "This plan is foolproof!"

"As long as the leader cooperates." Alexander added. "But then you convinced me without too much effort."

"Okay, then." Lex seemed impatient. "Derek needs a time and a place. Can anyone tell him?"

Kibble scratched his cheek. "Let's see, the Chinese civil war ended in 1949. Chiang had to vacate southern China and took over Taiwan. I'd say if we arrived in October of 1949, he would definitely be there."

Derek nodded. "Good so far. We just need a place." "Yes, yes." Kibble reassured him. "It was in northern Taiwan. Try Taipei."

"Got it!" Derek exclaimed. "I'll program a trip to there."

"Hold on!" Lex held her hands up. "Are you guys forgetting that you are now thinking about original earth history? This is the parallel universe, or whatever you call it, that we are living in!"

Everyone looked at Kibble, who briefly twirled his mustache, but then quickly spoke. "Yes, we live in a parallel time thread, but history on this side has mostly followed the other pretty close. In fact, I've studied this topic, and know it's nearly identical."

Derek stood up and walked to the C2 for programming. Alexander stood and brushed off his pants. "Well, let's make a go of it!"

8

The buffalo were still grazing in the same peaceful spot. But the time travelers were headed where it probably wouldn't be as serene. All were buckled in. But before leaving, Alexander reached into a compartment. "We will probably have to use these as soon as we get there." He hesitated. "Even though we want to be friends with them." He passed out scanners to all, for the purpose of not being fired upon. "We are pretty sure Chiang lived close to Taipei. That's as exact as we can get for now."

Derek flipped some switches and tapped his keyboard a few times. "Here we go." He looked around. No one spoke, so he flipped the go switch to start the cycle. Spinning slowed down and stopped, placing them in the middle of a field!

"This is 1948 in Taipei, Taiwan." Derek announced. Alexander peered out the window. "Not much to see. Let's fly around for a while to gain some perspective."

As Derek started the engine, Alexander continued. "This aircraft does have built in scanners."

Derek nodded. "And we can shoot down surface to air missiles." He lifted off smoothly, straight up into the air, and continued to 500 feet. Many things came into view, including the city of Taipei, off to the left.

"Go near the city." Alexander ordered. "Remember our goal is to speak with Chiang Kai-shek. When we meet opposition, scan their weapons, and then land."

Derek nodded, gliding effortlessly toward the city. Kibble sat behind the pilot, nervously twisting his mustache. Ed was next to him, enjoying the ride. He appeared as enthralled as a kid on a carnival ride. Lex was not afraid but did seem irritated that they were making this more complicated than need be.

Alexander sat in the copilot seat, calm and in control. He had fastened his trusty sword to his side and was ready for anything.

The fields got smaller, and the houses grew closer together, as they flew nearer and nearer to the city. More people appeared on the roads. Most stopped and stared at the odd-looking aircraft above them.

Soon soldiers began to appear in ever increasing numbers. Derek pushed on, not letting anything bother him. It didn't take long to get to the center of town.

Tall cement and brick buildings were everywhere. Crowds of soldiers occupied the streets and sidewalks. Soon the military became hostile. They started shooting their rifles at the C2.

"That's our cue!" Alexander's voice bore intensity. "Derek, you've got to scan them!" Derek calmly lowered his altitude and grabbed the swivel scanner on the control panel. He aimed and pulled the trigger at the crowds of soldiers below who were shooting at him. The guns became silent, and the C2 flew low, ten feet above the street. He suddenly stepped on it, zooming back up to 500 feet.

He glanced at Alexander. "I thought since no one speaks Chinese, we should try and find the president's palace.

Alexander nodded. "You assumed I couldn't speak it, but it's probably one of the dialects I learned when I was young."

"Oh, I didn't know." Derek bore a surprised expression.

"However," Alexander continued, "it wouldn't be a good idea to land in the street. Whether I speak the language or not, they are likely to shoot us if we land."

Derek began searching for anything that could be Chiang's residence. "Okay, everyone watch for anything that could be his home."

9

The C2 flew all around Taipei for an hour, finding nothing that resembled a president's palace. They had nearly come full circle when they noticed an airport. Parked on the open pavement were scores of military aircraft. "Looks like we hit the jackpot." Derek exclaimed.

Alexander leaned forward. "It might be an idea to land here and try to get directions to his place."

A chuckle came from the back seats where Ed was amused. "Well, that ought to open up a can of worms."

Derek took that as an order and started making preparations for a landing. As he decreased altitude, he saw activity on the pavement.

Soldiers were scurrying around. Alexander looked over his shoulder. "Have the scanners ready. In fact, we should start scanning now before they shoot at us."

At 50 feet the landing site was surrounded, and all rifles were pointed upward. Alexander had had enough. "Okay, everyone, scan the weapons below us. Shoot through the windows, so we don't scan ourselves."

They soon could see the soldiers trying to fire at them, but their guns were jammed. They became confused and checked their weapons.

"Derek!" Alexander prepared to disembark. "Shoot out some smoke grenades before we land. When we land, be ready with the swivel gun in case things go badly."

Smoke grenades dropped next to the circle of riflemen, belching noxious fumes of smoke. The soldiers retreated just as the C2 touched down.

Alexander spoke before stepping outside. "All of you stay here and keep scanning to shut down all weapons. I will see if we can talk to the president."

He then opened the door and got out. Smoke was still thick, as he walked in front of the C2, and up close to the soldiers. He raised one arm, thinking hard about the Mandarin language he learned as a young student.

Choosing his words carefully, he spoke. "I wish to speak to the president. I wish to be friends."

The soldiers appeared highly apprehensive...not knowing whether to stand or run. Alexander was unsure of his mastery of the language, or if it was the correct language.

Finally, one of the soldiers stepped forward and said something. "Come with me. I will take you to him."

Alexander nodded. "Let me speak to my friends, then I will join you."

He stepped over to the open door of the C2, and popped his head in. "You follow us from overhead and join me when we get there."

Derek agreed, so Alexander quickly closed the door, and joined the party of soldiers. The C2 then rose above the crowd, hovering closely, as if to protect Alexander.

The crowd of soldiers moved with Alexander toward a parking lot next to the runway. The leader invited him to ride in a military truck with him, as two other vehicles joined the travel party.

As the C2 hovered, the three-car party went onto the main highway and started their journey. They were not in a hurry. One of the two men in the back seat had a radio and was consulting with someone about meeting somewhere.

Soon they turned onto a smaller road, and then an even smaller one lane paved road. They shortly arrived at a large stone and mortar house. Pulling into a circular driveway, all three vehicles parked.

The leader was not treating Alexander like a prisoner, but rather a guest. They all got out of the truck at the same time and walked toward the house.

10

Two guards stood outside the door, but everyone, including Alexander, filed right past them.

Inside, the house appeared more like a president's palace. A plush carpet covered the floor of a hallway that led to a large, elegantly designed room. Velvet covered couches and chairs formed a circle.

Standing beside one chair was a man who appeared to be the president himself. He was bald and was dressed in a finely decorated military uniform.

He wore white gloves; one of which gripped a sword that hung at his side. The two soldiers that accompanied Alexander suddenly stood at attention and saluted him. He briskly returned the salutes and spoke. "At ease."

He looked directly at Alexander, introducing himself. "I am President Chiang Kai-shek. May I ask who you are?"

Alexander broke a faint smile. "I am Alexander. You may know me as Alexander the Great."

The president's face lost color and reflected confusion. "Gentlemen, please have a seat."

They sat, and he followed suit. He gazed at Alexander again before talking. "Sir, would you explain who you really are, and why you are here?"

Alexander nodded. "Of course. I realize that this sounds impossible, but I really was born in 323 BC. I am working with a group of time travelers, who right now are in their aircraft outside."

Chiang looked befuddled. "Before I go look, please tell me what it is you want with me."

Alexander flashed a serious look at him. "We just want to help you." He folded his hands. "You see, we know you have been fighting a war with Mao Zedong, and the communists. We also know that we are able to defeat him, and we will set you up as the Emperor of China."

Chiang's eyes widened. He was speechless for a moment, then cleared his throat and recovered. "Of course, this is what I have always been fighting for, but I am having trouble believing what you are saying."

Alexander held up one hand. "Please, sir. Allow me to prove this to you before you make a decision."

He glanced out the window. "Let us go outside, and I will show you the time travel machine, and explain how we will defeat Mao Zedong."

Chiang still appeared to be in shock, but he nodded. "Okay, let's go."

The four men stood, and Alexander took the lead toward the door, followed by Chiang. Opening the front door, he stepped out, and followed the sidewalk a few feet. Chiang kept close behind him.

Both men looked into the sky, where the C2 was close, and easily seen. Alexander waved for it to come and land near the house. He looked at Chiang. "Four of my friends are in the aircraft."

As the C2 came softly in for a landing, he looked seriously again at Chiang. "This aircraft can disable Mao's weapons just by pushing a button. You can ask your men. We disabled their weapons when they tried to fire on us."

The C2 was now resting on the ground. Chiang looked at Alexander as he answered. "I would like to see this great weapon killer." He glanced at the C2. "And I would like to see this time machine."

11

Alexander walked with Chiang to the C-2, where the doors opened, and out came the crew to meet him.

Speaking Mandarin up to this time, he asked Chiang in English, "I know your wife speaks English, but do you?"

The Taiwanese president's eyes brightened as he smiled at Alexander. "This is a great passion for me to speak English. My wife is the best teacher I know." He then bowed to the C-2 crew, who respectfully returned the favor.

Alexander got right to the point. "What battle was the most important for you? One that you lost, but you feel you should have won."

Chiang, who spoke English with a strong accent, didn't hesitate with an answer. "The battle of Peking. When I lost this battle, I had to go into exile in Taiwan."

Alexander placed a hand on Chiang's arm. "Let's go correct that outcome right now. Come with us."

Chiang hesitated, as though he were doubtful or afraid. But he nodded and followed Alexander to the C-2 co-pilot door.

Chiang felt that this was dangerous getting to an aircraft with unfamiliar people. But he was overcome by the enchantment of a second chance to win the civil war.

He jumped in and sat down. The crew quickly followed suit. Alexander sat behind Chiang, while Derek was in the driver's seat, and the others came along for the ride.

"To Peking," Alexander directed the mission information to Derek, "on the day of the battle in 1949."

Derek looked it up on the built-in encyclopedia and noted the date and time of the battle. It took him a minute to program it into the transporter.

Alexander turned around to deliver a final message before departure. "We will identify the enemy's position, and then use all our scanners to decommission their weapons.

He turned to Chiang. "We are going back to the battle of Peking to shut down the Red Army's weapons. When we return from this trip, you will be the ruler of all China. It will be that you have won the battle of Peking, and then won every other battle.

Do you understand what I am saying?" Chiang nodded. "I understand." He spoke as if to say, "I'll believe it when I see it." But the tone of his voice still reflected hope.

Derek powered up, and lifted straight up, slowed down, and then shot forward to an upward incline. After reaching 1,000 feet, he came to a stop, hovering silently.

He poked at the keyboard briefly and looked at Chiang. "Here we go. It will just take a minute to get there."

He reached to the control panel and flipped a switch. Spinning commenced outside the C-2 windows. Visibility ceased momentarily. After about 30 seconds, a distinct boom ripped through the cockpit, and all was clear.

Chiang looked out the window to the ground. He could see Peking under attack. He saw his own forces defending against the invaders. But he also clearly realized his side was losing the battle.

"We must do something now!" Desperation emanated from his voice. Derek nodded. "This is it, folks! Make sure you distinguish between enemy and friend. The enemy is moving toward the city to attack. Start scanning as soon as you get a good view."

He then powered the C-2 into a dive toward the invading Red Army. Grabbing the swivel scanner, he engaged the attackers. "Now!" He yelled.

All the passengers with scanners aimed through the windows at their targets. The Reds saw them coming, and turned their weapons toward the C-2, including heavy machine guns and anti-aircraft weapons. But these weapons never fired a shot. They were jammed, and the soldiers could be seen tinkering with them trying to fix them.

Derek then circled around, heading once again toward the offensive forces. Coming in low, he released two missiles in front of the enemy. The explosions were so massive that the entire army turned and ran as fast as they could go.

Chiang, whose eyes were as wide as saucers, could not keep it in any longer. He yelled and pumped his fist into the air. Turning to Derek, he reached out and slapped his back. "Now I believe!" Derek smiled, as he leveled off and streaked over the heads of the retreating army. Making sure they were all on the same page, he did a U-turn back to the city.

Everyone saw the Nationals, led by Chiang's counterpart, in full pursuit of Mao's communists. The crew of the C-2 cheered along with Chiang, at the sight of their enemies running. And so ended this battle of Peking in January of 1949.

12

Alexander sipped tea at the kitchen table, joined by the other four time-travelers. Chiang had given them a large government house to stay in, at least for the night. He had also given them a generous amount of money to live on while they stayed.

"You know," Alexander remarked, as he sat his teacup down, "whoever shops for food needs to try to find coffee. I like it much better."

A chuckle came from Ed's direction. "I'll be sure I've got that on my list." He eyed his own cup suspiciously. "I'm with you on that."

Lex shook her head. "You guys don't know what's good for you." Setting her own half empty cup down, she scoffed. "Who cares about tea and coffee, anyway? What's our next adventure?"

Alexander took another sip of bland tea and held it out as though he were offering a toast. "This should be wine," he joked, "but I still offer a toast to the recapture of Nanjing and Canton today."

"So, I see." Lex moaned. "No rest and relaxation today."

Kibble laughed. "I really think we'll staying on the mainland tonight. We'll take those two cities and stay somewhere till the next day."

"Oh yes." Ed agreed, while shaking his head. "It might take several days to recapture all of China."

Alexander carried on the thought. "When we're done, we'll check the future for positive effect."

Lex sighed. "I don't think we'll ever find as perfect a setup as we just had the last two years."

Kibble stepped to the sink and poured his entire cup of tea down the drain. "We know very well by now," he looked at Lex, "that we'll take the best situation that is available."

"We know the drill." Derek snorted. "We just need to get ourselves into a good position. We may not be kings and queens, but we'll be safe and happy."

A knock at the front door broke the mood. "First things first." Alexander stood to answer the door. "It's time to go to work right now."

Chiang was at the door anxious to get started with taking his country back. "Good morning to you all!" He burst out with his strange English accent. Alexander nodded and smiled. "Good morning to you." He motioned to the table for the group to come. "We are ready to go if you are."

Together they walked toward the C-2. Everyone stood and followed to be witnesses of Chiang's miraculous resurrection of the defeated.

Everyone buckled in and waited for Derek to program the trip to Nanjing. Alexander passed out the scanners, and in-serviced Chiang on their use. He was happy to actually use one of these 'weapon killers' for himself.

The C-2 engine started, and the aircraft effortlessly lifted off, powering swiftly to 500 feet.

"It will be the same routine as yesterday." Alexander instructed. "Wait until we run into the military. Then we will scan together, taking out all their weapons instantly. They will have no chance against us."

Everyone held their scanners in readiness. Derek announced it. "Here we go!" He flipped the switch and started the cycle, while the C-2 hovered. Then they suddenly appeared in Nanjing.

"Move up to that airport ahead." Alexander ordered. Upon arrival, they just sat, waiting for some opposition.

13

All was deathly quiet. Nothing seemed to be happening. This made everyone nervous.

Lex knew it was not normal. She searched out her window, and noticed a man standing next to something. She squinted, straining to see, and suddenly gasped. "It's a missile!" She brought up her scanner to disable it, but it fired an instant before she could.

"Missile coming!" She shouted. Derek didn't hesitate. He pushed a button labeled S.A.M.. The C-2 fired a missile of its own that searched out the one from the ground. Immediately there was a massive explosion in midair.

The crew was shocked and began scanning all around. "I think we're easier targets when we are stationary."

Alexander expressed a change of heart to Derek. "Move around so we can search for targets." The C-2 glided across the city noting the enemy's location and scanning them off the map.

It didn't take long to scan out the entire area. Mass confusion reigned below, while the crew above was elated.

Flying all over Nanjing, they knocked out every weapon in sight. Derek then transported the C-2 to Canton, where they went through the same process. But this time it was quicker and easier. All weapons were disabled, and SAMs were prioritized.

Chiang clenched both fists and sported the victory sign. Everyone laughed, and high-fived each other.

Momentarily, Alexander made an announcement. "We've now taken all three cities, but without forces on the ground, it will not be safe to land. He then addressed Chiang.

"How long will it take to transport troops to these three cities?" Chiang grinned, and nodded vigorously. "They will start today, going by air and sea. In a few days, we will have them under control."

"Very well", Alexander was satisfied. "Derek", take us back to Taipei. We will continue the quest tomorrow."

14

The next morning, everyone, including Chiang, met at their humble kitchen table. The main topic was how to progress daily to retake the country.

It was agreed to take 2 or 3 cities a day until the entire country was theirs. It was a simple war of attrition caused by disabling all of their weapons.

Everyone agreed to continue weapons shutdown, while Chiang's army was repopulating as fast as they could. The group went out again and again.

At the end, it took 28 days to capture 56 cities. The daily grind took its toll on the flight crew, and all were dragging their feet...except Chiang, that is. He grew more excited each day.

The army, air force, and navy struggled to occupy so many cities. But they were still making progress and were maintaining the upper hand all over the land.

The crew sat around the same table again, after 28 days. Chiang was missing, having more than he could handle with the reoccupation. No one showed signs of energy reserve, but Alexander happily sipped his favorite drink...coffee.

"We are now on the next phase of repairing the breech of our world." He made eye contact all around the circle.

As he took another sip, Kibble picked up the slack. "This will undoubtedly include a check of the year 2030." Alexander nodded. "That's the first place to check, considering what we just did in China."

Lex quickly sat her cup on the table with a loud clink. "You guys had better realize something right now." She made sure everyone was paying attention. "Since we fixed China in 1949, that's going to change all the good we did in 2028 to 2030." No one spoke, so she continued. "All I mean is it's going to be a different world, maybe not so good."

After a moment, Kibble responded. "Sure, we expect to see a different world. But hopefully a more secure one than we left."

Alexander smiled and nodded. "The only way we'll find out is to try it. We did what we could to make it better now. We'll see what the far-reaching effects are."

Ed half grinned as he raised his cup. "Here's to after breakfast."

Everyone trudged out to the C-2 after the meal, and slowly took their seats. Derek punched in the coordinates to their former familiar surroundings and took to the air.

At 1,000 feet, he hovered, waiting for the call. It came right away from Alexander. "Okay, take us to the capital building. Be ready to leave in an instant if there is any danger."

A flip of the switch triggered the sequence, which spun out, and popped them into a different world of 2030.

Instead of the capital building, below were housing developments. Brows wrinkled, and eyes widened. "Well, we definitely changed a lot of things." Derek spoke first.

"Be careful." Alexander busily surveyed out every window. "It may not be friendly. We don't know. Let's explore the area and see if there's a place to land."

Derek soared over scores of neighborhoods, until breaking into a clearing that appeared to be a park. He glanced at Alexander. "This be Okay?" "Yes," Alexander nodded, "let's try it."

Derek maneuvered toward a clearing in the trees, gently descending until the wheels touched on the grass.

"Looks friendly enough." Alexander spoke as he opened the door. "I'll get out for a minute." He jumped out and stepped a few paces, letting the door swing open. Close by he saw children playing on swing sets, climbing bars, and slide. A few parents were sitting on benches staring at him, but no one ran. Then a car door opened, and out stepped a well-dressed man.

15

The well-dressed man walked slowly toward the C-2, as if he were unsure about it. Alexander stood his ground, just to see how the man would react. He kept walking, and went right up to Alexander, holding out his hand in a gesture of friendliness.

"Hello, my name is Chad Power." Alexander shook his hand cautiously. "Alexander", he returned curtly. "Wow!" The man seemed truly amazed. "Nice looking sword there. Mind if I ask where you folks are from?"

Alexander stood, placing hands on hips. "We are time travelers. But we are here as friends." Chad's mouth gaped open, queuing Alexander to continue. "We are from the United American Republics." This made no impression on Chad, so Alexander asked a question.

"Let me ask you...what is the name of this country?" Chad hesitated for a moment. "Um, this is the United American Republics. And I'm the mayor of this city, so if I can help you with anything, I'd be glad to."

Alexander scratched his head and stared briefly at the man. "Do you have a few minutes to chat with us?"

"Certainly." Chad answered, as the two men gravitated toward the C-2.

Alexander popped his head in. "Let's all get out for a brief discussion." Everyone happily climbed out to stretch their legs.

Standing around the aircraft, Alexander made an introduction. "This is Chad, the mayor of this town. And these are my flight crew members, from the 21st century, except for me."

"By the way," the visitor kept his gaze on Alexander, "And what time period do you hail from?"

"The ancient past." Alexander promptly returned. He fastened his eyes on Chad. "Do you remember a historical character named Alexander the Great?" Without waiting for an answer, he concluded. "That's me."

Chad leaned against the side of the aircraft. "Unbelievable." He shook his head. "This is story book material."

He stood up straight. "So, what brings you here?" Kibble jumped in. "We were trying to improve the future, which is now. Original history in 1949 had the communists winning the civil war of China. We helped Chiang Kai-shek win the war, and we are checking this country to see if America has benefited."

Chad rubbed his forehead with the back of his hand. "Wow!" He looked at Kibble and Alexander. "Well, I can tell you it didn't work. The Chinese have become so strong that they are now dictating how our economy goes.

And our own country is now a police state."

Alexander and Kibble looked at each other. Chad continued. "Mr. Alexander, this is not what you are looking for." He stepped closer, his body language brimming with excitement. "But whatever you do, please take me with you! I know I can be of assistance."

Alexander blinked, nodded his head, and squeezed Chad's upper arms. "Don't worry. We have plenty of room in this aircraft."

He then turned and focused on the crew. "Well, what options do we have now?"

Silence reigned, but finally Lex spoke her mind. "I don't see that we have any choice. We have to go back and fix it. I know the last one didn't work out, but we didn't put ourselves into it. All we did was shut down their weapons."

Kibble agreed. "She's got a point. We must put boots on the ground and employ some effort."

Ed held up one hand. "I believe we should go back far enough to really make an impression. We need a grass roots movement."

Derek nodded vigorously. "Modern weapons have more of an impact on the psyche of primitive people." "This sounds pretty convincing." Alexander spoke while holding his arms and shoulders in a shrugging gesture.

Lex was there with another answer. "It should be before guns were invented. Like we did before in America...around 1500."

16

"Alright, folks." Alexander opened the C-2 door. "Let's get in and buckle up." As everyone filed in, Chad noticed two police cars pulling up. This made him extremely nervous.

"Better get a move on, friends. We've got company!" He dived in himself and quickly strapped into a seat. Everyone else did the same.

As the police jumped out of their cars and began running, Derek was firing up the engine. He watched them carefully. As they reached for their guns, he blasted them with the scanner. As they pulled the triggers, and their guns jammed, he lifted off the ground.

The C-2 rocketed straight up, and all the playground kids and adults stared with gaping jaws. He kept rising to 2,000 feet, then stopped to program the trip.

Derek knew he had to work fast, and sure enough, jet fighters appeared on the horizon. He flipped the switch, and soon saw the puffs of smoke from distant missile fire.

He knew it was going to be close, so he fired two anti-SAM missiles, which turned out to be wise. Two big explosions occurred just before the time sequence. Everyone jumped, but had no time to recuperate, as the scenery faded and blurred.

Chad was not prepared for this, and began struggling, thinking a crash was occurring. Ed grabbed his arm and clamped down. "It's Okay," he consoled, "we're doing fine."

The C-2 seemed to pop through a channel and spurt out into a world of evergreen trees and bright sun.

Derek gained control of the C-2 and looked around for a place land. "This is 1500." He called over his shoulder. He glanced at Alexander. "We are landing, right?"

"Find a spot." Alexander spoke with a nod. "We need to talk."

The C-2 softly descended until it touched down on a sandy beach along the Atlantic Ocean. The terrain gradually angled upward, where not far away was the start of a thick forest.

Alexander wasted no time. Turning around in his seat, he delivered an order. "Kibble, pass out the laser rifles." Quickly Kibble unbuckled and opened a compartment behind the seats. He hustled six rifles out and passed them around.

While everyone was unloading, Kibble opened another compartment and grabbed six prepared lunches in paper bags. The group stood on the sand next to the C-2, taking in the beauty and fresh air.

"Okay." Alexander broke the silence while grabbing a lunch sack. "We don't know what's out there, so have the rifles ready."

Derek leaned over and showed Chad the safety. Alexander smiled and went on. "As long as we are ready for any kind of hostility, we'll be fine. These rifles could take out a grizzly bear."

He sat down on the sand and opened his lunch. Everyone followed suit. Lex no sooner got seated cross-legged, than she had a point to make.

She looked at everyone in the circle and began speaking her mind. "I'm not sure what all you are going to talk about, but I want to get one thing straight right now."

She reached into her bag and pulled out a rice cake. She silently looked around at every face. "Ed and Chad, you weren't here, but the rest of us were. We spent two years going from Canada to Florida, and back. Now that was all primitive living, which I hate, and I won't do it again."

She brushed her hair back with one hand. "Look, there must be a way to go back to when we did it the first time and make changes where they're needed."

Kibble squelched a laugh just in time. "You took the words right out of my mouth. We're just going to have to find the right time thread to lead us all the way to Dennis Carrigan and his kingdom."

17

"Yes!" Alexander shouted as he drew his sword and thrust it into the ground. The handle was quivering as he spoke. "Exactly right! Since we're here now, it might be easier to fit into the right time thread."

Derek suddenly had a thought. "We were here the first time in 1500 AD. I can also get us to the key cities we visited. I think we should go to the city of Grange town just after the battle. That would confirm that we are in the correct time thread."

Kibble's eyes lit up. He thrust one hand into the air in excitement. "Derek, I should have paid for your education long ago!"

Alexander smiled and nodded in agreement. After lunch, the time travelers loaded up in preparation for the trip to Grange town.

Chad was starting to feel at home just by keeping his eyes and ears open. No one really had much opportunity to talk to him yet.

Derek programmed the trip and spoke to the group. "We are heading for Grange town on the day of the battle in 1500. We'll be starting from the air, so we'll take off now."

He started the engine and lifted off to 1,000 feet. Flipping the switch, he started the time sequence, which finished with a boom, spitting them out into a raging battle.

Everyone watched from the air with great interest. People were dying in front of them, and the battle saw each side waxing and waning. The settlers had the upper hand until the natives mounted an attack, forcing a steady retreat. Suddenly reinforcements came in from the side, changing the complexion of the battle.

Then a helicopter came roaring in, and all hell broke loose. The natives cut and ran on a westbound trail. The helicopter came after them, shooting rockets and machine guns nearby, just to incite fear.

As the time travelers sat watching in the C-2, Derek shook his head. "I have no idea why I didn't see the C-2 while I was flying the helicopter."

Kibble pursed his lips and looked glassy eyed through the window. "Derek, it's one of the mysteries of time travel."

Alexander broke the mood. "Okay, next stop 2028. We're going to talk to Dennis Carrigan or our counterparts about keeping the shutdown system away from our enemies."

Derek programmed the trip and looked around. "Here we go!"

Everyone was ready, but no one knew what to expect. The sequence took them and exploded them into 2028. Heads pressed against the windows.

"This is the Capitol building, and everything looks the same!" Derek announced, excitement swelling in his voice.

"Take it down to the front lawn." The order came calmly from Alexander. Over the edge went the C-2, slowly descending until it landed softly on the lawn.

Alexander looked around. "Okay, Kibble and I are going in to see what or who we run into. We'll be back soon."

The two men exited and walked together up the cement stairs like they had done so many times before. When they reached the front door, they looked at each other. Kibble spoke first.

"You realize that we probably won't be able to speak to our counterparts. But I should be able to speak to yours, and you to mine." Alexander smiled and opened the glass door. "Let's go."

18

Alexander and Kibble walked to the elevator. People were busy in their offices or walking around. Several greeted them as they always had done before. The elevator door closed, and silently carried them up to the top...the 5th floor.

As the elevator opened, security guards stood on both sides. Both bore shocked and amazed expressions.

The visitors didn't let that deter them. They stepped forward across a wide floor to where Alexander's office was. At the door, Alexander spoke quietly to Kibble. "You go in by yourself to start out with. If all goes well, you can invite me in."

Kibble nodded. "Sounds like it just might work." Alexander took a seat in one of the cushioned chairs outside the door.

Kibble stepped up and knocked before entering, as was his custom. Swinging the door inward, he stepped confidently in. Closing the door behind him, he could see Alexander standing and staring out the window.

To his relief, his own counterpart was not there. He prepared to speak to the Alexander he had known over two years ago. The one who had just started this job as king.

It took a moment to think of something to say. "I've got news." Alexander turned toward the door. His eyes widened. "Back so soon?" He then broke out with a patented belly laugh.

"You left ten minutes ago, and now you're back. With totally different clothes on! What's happening?" He stepped closer and studied Kibble for a moment. "Huh! Your hair is different too!" Kibble held up both hands, flashing a genuine grin.

"It's like I said. I've got news." Alexander folded his arms. "This should be interesting."

Kibble nodded. "It is. And tragic at the same time." He paused. "You see, I'm from two years into the future."

Alexander was taken back… his face took on a stunned appearance. He looked at Kibble. "Now it makes more sense. I can deal with this. Obviously, it must be pretty important."

Kibble, expressing great conviction with his hands, offered an explanation. "In two years if you don't do anything, your enemies will develop their own weapon shutdown system. With most of the world against you, this country will be overrun or nuked. I'm not sure which, because we left just before it happened."

Alexander pulled his sword from its sheath, examined it, and fastened his eyes on Kibble. "So, what do you suggest we do?"

Kibble opened his mouth to answer, but the door creaked and swung open. Taking three steps into the room was Alexander, the older version. He made eye contact with his counterpart, who stood, clearly entranced by this experience.

"Here is what you must do. Do not be softhearted. Occupy every country. Monitor all science projects. You have to run the world, and don't be lax. Then everyone can live in peace." He turned to leave but hesitated for a second. "Good luck."

Alexander the younger version suddenly nodded and smiled. "Thank you for the warning and advice. We will do as you say." A faint grin appeared on the older man's face, as he stepped out the door.

Kibble nervously twisted the tip of his mustache before speaking. "I hope the next two years are better for you than they were for us." He started to leave. Alexander held up his hands. "What will you do now?" Kibble grinned. "Try to find another Utopia." He paused. "I hope we've saved this one." Alexander gritted his teeth. "We'll make it work."

19

Kibble and Alexander exited the building and joined the C-2 crew. All were anxious to hear the results of the visit. "Don't keep it to yourselves." Lex implored. "Who did you talk to?"

Kibble chuckled. "I believe we were successful. I had a short discussion with Alexander's counterpart. And both Alexanders spoke to each other without any interference. Clear as a bell."

"Exactly!" Alexander chipped in. "And he's going to follow our advice about beefing up security, and not allowing any weapons shutdown research."

"Well, chalk up another world save!" Lex celebrated. "Just wish we could live in it."

"You can be happy for your counterpart." Ed smiled. "I hope mine lives happily ever after."

"I'm guessing it'll be up to us to find another utopia." Chad offered some word for thought.

Alexander laughed. "And that is what we will do. But let's get up in the air first. Can't stay here."

Derek responded quickly, and the C-2 flew straight up like an elevator. At 3,000 feet he stopped and hovered the craft.

"Just to finish our discussion," Alexander continued, "we will have to search the future for a time and place of our liking."

Derek spoke up. "This may be a good time to tell you about a discovery I've recently made." All eyes fixed on him. "We can now travel back and forth from one time thread to another. I can number and label them for easy reference."

"Wow!" Lex sounded amazed as she leaned forward. Does that mean we can find other time threads that we've never been in before?"

Derek nodded emphatically. "That's right. And get this...it looks like there are an unlimited variety of worlds out there to discover. Don't know if there are any utopias, or if they're all night-mares, but they are there for us to explore!"

Kibble was astounded. "How did you discover this?"

Derek shrugged. "Just by fooling around with the programming." He pointed at the screen. "You can see all the possibilities popping up whenever I program a trip. I always thought it was static, but these are time threads!" He shook his head. "We won't know what any of these are like until we try them."

"Kind of scary," Chad piped up, "but it does sound exciting."

"What we need to decide," Lex seemed thrilled, "is should we stay in this time period, or try earlier or later ones."

Ed laughed. "I think it's a crap shoot. We have no idea what any of them are going to look like."

Kibble elaborated. "I think that since Derek discovered this, he should make the first choice."

"Huh?" Derek laughed. "That way you can blame a bad choice on me. Sounds like a real deal for you guys!"

"Still, I'd like you to pick one." Alexander added. "You are the most qualified to start."

Derek stared at the screen and tapped his fingers on the control panel. "Well, there's no info to base my decision on, so I'm going to have to just pick one. I will keep them all in modern time periods."

Ed anxiously interjected. "Wait, Derek! I think we should concentrate on earlier time periods. Not primitive, but lesser technology gives us a better chance to dominate with our shutdown system, and this fancy aircraft we're flying."

Derek acknowledged. "Yes, I follow. I think that this is a splendid idea that would give us a great advantage."

Lex pushed across another thought. "If you want to dominate, how about using the shutdown system during WW2. Say somewhere around 1942."

"What a proposition!" Kibble marveled. "They needed victory in the worst way! We could sure carve ourselves out a place in society."

Derek looked around. "Does everyone agree with this idea?"

The main consensus was positive. Alexander gave the nod. "I don't know a lot about your history, but everyone seems to like the idea."

20

Derek started programming the trip. "I'm just picking one of these many time threads. We'll try it, but we can return in a hurry with one click of the mouse, or stroke of the enter key."

With that, he initiated the trip. As they popped into the new reality, Derek looked around. "Oh, by the way, I forgot to mention that we are in the war zone. We're now just off-shore from Great Britain."

Lex was shocked. "What? Are you trying to get us killed?"

"We'll be Okay." Derek hastily replied. "We're going to fly under the radar."

He quickly dropped altitude from 3,000 feet, and then slowly swung to 20 feet above the ocean. Soon the C-2 reached shore, flying just above the rooftops. Derek continued to skid from house to field to street, until an airfield loomed ahead. As a pilot, Derek could think quickly, and didn't need someone barking orders at him. Everyone now seemed to realize this.

Once the C-2 reached the airfield, he slowed down, and lowered his altitude to five feet. He whizzed up to the headquarters building and made a soft landing before drawing much attention.

As the crew peeked out the windows, they could see row upon row of B-17 bombers, accompanied by scores of British Spitfire fighter planes.

The C-2 was already attracting attention. Alexander started to get out. "If it's safe, we'll all get out, but first Kibble and I will see if we are accepted. Have the scanners in your hands. Watch for danger from friend or foe."

The two men cautiously opened the doors and stepped out. They slowly walked toward the headquarters entrance. Airmen came wandering in from every direction, wondering what the odd-looking aircraft was all about.

Kibble and Alexander walked into the building, looking for someone to talk to. One of the doors was partially open and was labeled "Commanding Officer". Alexander looked at Kibble, as he knocked and swung the door open.

Inside stood a distinguished looking British officer who was talking to a seated group of about 20 pilots.

A look of consternation came over his face. "Wait outside! No reporters allowed until after the briefing!" Alexander and Kibble stood side by side.

Kibble raised one hand. "We are not reporters, and I think you will be interested to know how we can help you."

The C.O. became angry. "Who let you in here? Confounded! We have a mission to prepare for!"

Alexander instinctively stepped forward, resting his left hand on his sword. He spoke with the authoritative voice of an emperor.

"Stop and listen! We have an aircraft that will win every battle for you without firing a shot." A wave of laughter rippled through the contingent of pilots. The C.O. was dumbstricken, and just stared at Alexander.

"I'm serious!" Alexander motioned toward the door with one hand. "It's right outside."

"Who are you, and where are you from?" An astonished look was pasted on the C.O.'s face.

Kibble jumped in. "I'm an American scientist, and this is Alexander, an experienced military leader."

Alexander cut in again. "We could tell you more, but you will want to see this great weapon first."

The C.O. shook his head. "You know, I can't believe you men are for real!" He looked at Alexander. "And what are you, a Roman centurion?"

Alexander smiled and motioned again toward the door. "First things first." He implored. The C.O. flashed a look of disgust to Alexander and Kibble. "This had better be good." He shuffled forward. As he stepped out the door, he froze when he saw the C-2. "Whatever is this contraption?"

Kibble and Alexander filed past him, followed by all of the inquisitive pilots. Ed and the rest of the time travelers hopped out of the aircraft. Kibble spoke up.

"This is Ed Worth. He is the inventor of the weapon." The C.O. glanced at Ed. "I am Colonel Dunn. So, what does this machine do?"

Ed stepped up to the colonel. "I didn't invent the aircraft. I invented the system. It's called the weapons shutdown system."

"How does it shut down enemy weapons?" Ed stood up straight and pulled down his shirt tail. "It has what's called a scanner. You can point it at, and scan any kind of weapon, and it's rendered useless. That is instantly, and permanently, until I reverse it with the same scanner."

Colonel Dunn looked at Ed. "I don't know who in the bloody hell you people are, but we'll definitely run a test on this!"

21

Ed reached into his trousers and pulled out a scanner. "This is the same weapon scanner that's in our aircraft. You just point it like a gun and pull the trigger. Works from any distance."

He handed the scanner to Colonel Dunn. Ed continued. "Why don't you send an aircraft up and let us scan it. Then you can see for yourself how well it works."

The Colonel shouted over his shoulder. "Leftenant Bicksly, take your plane up for a gun test, and come right back!" The Leftenant jumped in and fired up the engine. He quickly took off and began circling around.

"Okay," Ed addressed the Colonel, "Aim the scanner at the aircraft, and pull the trigger." Nothing seemed to happen. Colonel Dunn looked at Ed. "What's wrong with this thing?"

Ed shook his head. "Nothing. It did work. Just wait." Just then the pilot radioed in, "Negative. Guns are jammed, returning to base."

"I'll be a pot-cracker!" The Colonel spouted off. "That crazy gizmo works!"

Ed handed the Colonel another scanner. "We have enough of these for every pilot to carry with him. They can be used successfully from inside the cockpit." He pointed to the C-2. "We'll go along with our aircraft. It has powerful built-in scanners." Facing the Colonel, he concluded. "You should never lose another aircraft, and you should shoot down every one of theirs from now on."

Colonel Dunn looked at Ed, Kibble, and Alexander. "Where in blazes did you people come from!?"

Alexander stepped forward, gesturing with his hands as he spoke. "Let's just say that all of us are Americans who want to end this war quickly. Will you let us help?" The Colonel rubbed his chin for a moment before answering. "Look here! We're running a mission in 30 minutes. The B17s and Lancasters will bomb a target in Germany. The Spitfires won't be able to reach the target before running out of fuel. Will your aircraft run out of fuel?"

"No." Kibble replied. "It's solar powered. We can stay with the bombers and disable everything they send up."

"Smashing!" The Colonel snapped a pair of gloves on his pant leg. "You folks wait here for 20 minutes. Then we will commence with the mission! We must finish our briefing. Back inside, gentlemen!"

The pilots edged toward the door, while the time travelers hung around the C-2. This aircraft was equipped with its own bathroom, running water, food, and supplies. The crew lounged until the British pilots came pouring out.

Alexander stood. "Looks like it's time to buckle in." Everyone scrambled to their seats. Colonel Dunn arrived, so Alexander and Kibble stepped out to meet him. He quickly delivered the information. "Here's the skinny. There are 100 bombers, and 25 fighters. But, as you know, the Spitfires will turn back before they reach Germany. Your aircraft will stay above the bomber groups to see better and avoid friendly fire."

Alexander and Kibble nodded. The Colonel began walking away. "Best of luck! We'll see you after the mission!"

Everyone was loading up and starting their engines. The two men returned to the C-2 and relayed the information to Derek. As Alexander buckled in, he continued. "It's a good idea to stay above the group. But do whatever is needed to in order to shut down enemy weapons."

"You got it!" Derek sounded confident. "We're goanna take 'em out!"

22

The noise was deafening, as 100 bombers lined up to take off. After them were the 25 fighters, whose job was to defend the bombers. The C-2 crew couldn't figure out why the spitfires even went along, if they would barely even reach the other side of the channel.

Derek, thinking as he prepared to fly, was convinced that was why the C-2 was so desperately needed.

The bombers continued to take to the sky, and soon Alexander gave the order. "Take us straight up and find your place over the group."

The C-2 silently shot up the elevator shaft and continued until Derek had a good view of where the bombers were. He flew forward at top speed, and quickly caught up with them.

Ed issued an important reminder. "Everyone; have your scanners ready. We don't know when we'll actually meet the enemy."

The crew seemed nervous. This was a different kind of warfare than they had previously experienced.

Lex began to feel slightly bored; and put out a question for anyone. "I am definitely not in my element here, but I would like to know where we are going."

"Well, from listening to Colonel Dunn," Kibble began, we are headed to the outskirts of Berlin."

Lex gasped. "You're kidding!"

Kibble nervously twisted his mustache. "Afraid not. It's about 1,700 miles round trip. So, the fighter planes will stay with us for 500 miles before they have to turn back."

Chad bore a perplexed expression. "Apparently, they haven't yet been retrofitted with extra gas tanks."

"Keep in mind," Derek offered, "that this is one of many time threads, which means that history may not follow exactly the way we knew it."

"That's scary." Lex lamented. "That means, in this time thread, Germany could have won the war."

"It's going to be different with us here." Ed sounded confident.

Not long after the bomber group reached land, Lex sounded the alarm. "Airplanes in the distance, to the right!"

Everyone squinted, and quickly saw them. Two large groups of fighters approaching their position in a hurry.

Alexander eyed Derek. "Be sure to cover them before they get to any of the bombers."

Derek turned right, heading straight for them. "Everyone! Scan them before they spread apart!" He reached down and grabbed the swivel scanner, waiting until the enemy got a little closer.

"Fire!" He yelled. He and the crew let them have it with a constant barrage of scanning. Then the second group swooped in, getting the same treatment.

The Messerschmitt's flew around out of control, taking fire from the bombers and spitfires. They then turned and tried to escape but were taking fire from many bombers and 25 fighters. It took only a minute for every one of them to disappear...casualties of war, thanks to the C-2.

The C-2 had no connection to the radio communication of the contingent, but the flight crew knew they were celebrating. Several aircraft tipped their wings back and forth in an expression of delight.

Not long after that, another group of bandits were spotted...about 30 BF 109s. These were generally known as the best of all fighters in the world.

They fearlessly zoomed to within striking distance of the expansive group of bombers.

"Now!" Ed shouted. "Before they separate, shoot!" Everyone scanned, including Derek with the C-2.

The same thing happened again. The attacking fighters started wobbling; and appeared very uncertain. Then they tried to turn around and escape. That's when everyone pounced on them. Bombers and Spitfires alike simply obliterated them. The helpless BF 109s were blown out of the sky. A few pilots managed to escape with parachutes, but not many. It was another total wipeout.

Colonel Dunn, who was in one of the bombers, celebrated by slapping the pilot and co-pilot on their backs. "That weapon is a beast! I say, we've already won the bloody war!"

23

The group continued for an hour with no attacks. Soon the C-2 crew noticed the Spitfires turning and heading back home. "This is it." Alexander announced. "We are on our own now."

Derek did some quick calculations. "London to Berlin is roughly 850 miles. It'll be an hour before we get there."

Kibble spoke up. "This means that we'll be their only escort. But we may run into large numbers in Berlin. We'll have to be fast with the scanners."

Ed was studying a group of B-17s below. "You know, I thought B-17s didn't enter the war until 1941."

Derek perked up. "True, but we're in one of many diversified time threads. In each one, events happened at different times, and in different ways."

Kibble added a bit of history. "Until 1942, the B-17s were flown by the Royal air force. That was about the time America entered the war. Not sure whether these chaps are British or American."

The bombing group met no resistance for the next 45 minutes. Then, suddenly it came. A mixed contingent of enemy aircraft came at them in great numbers.

All the gunners in bomber turrets gave their best effort. But it wouldn't have been enough had the C-2 not been there.

Derek flew quickly toward the main source of the German Luftwaffe. "Scan, and don't stop scanning until we've done away with them all!"

Everyone went wild with their scanners, covering all 360 degrees of window in the C-2.

Bombers were taking hits, but still staying in the fight. The onslaught nearly overwhelmed them, but the fast action of the scanners saved the day. The C-2 crew finally appeared to have decommissioned the enemy.

The attacking fighters could not shoot their weapons and were defenseless. They could be seen wavering, as the pilots tried to unjam their guns. This was the cue for the bombers to pick them off. The fighters tried to turn around, but too many guns were aimed at them, and they were blown out of the sky. Colonel Dunn, in one of the Lancasters whooped and hollered, while pumping his fists. "To bloody hell with those blasted Nazis!"

The bomber group settled back into formation and continued their mission. Derek squinted. "We are coming up on Berlin."

"Watch for more surprises!" Alexander barked out the warning.

Soon the city came into view. Then the surprises came, but the scanners kept pace with them, and they were shot down.

The bombers had now reached their targets and were releasing their loads. Flak guns on the ground wreaked havoc on the group, blowing holes in their fuselages and wings.

Derek dived toward the flak guns. "Scan everything on the ground!" He yelled. Seeing a large group of guns ahead, he opted to shoot a missile at them. Within seconds, the entire area was one massive plume of smoke.

He flew quickly back to the top to avoid bombs dropping on him. Everyone continued scanning weapons on the ground.

Another large squadron of Bf 109s came at them. The scanners were now getting fast and made quick work of them.

The bomber targets were hit, and the big group of planes turned and headed for home. No more fighters or flak were incoming. It was a strange feeling for Colonel Dunn and his pilots to serenely fly back over Berlin. The city had no more fight to offer.

24

The C-2's flight back was high-spirited, after their sweeping victories. Alexander was optimistic about the possibility of staying in this time period. "Before this is over, we are going to be well known heroes."

Ed's first reaction was barely controlled laughter. "No disrespect, Alexander, but that probably starts now." He paused for a moment. "Oh, not that I have the least desire to be a hero. I just want a good lab, and the time to work in it."

Alexander pasted a sly smile, as he slowly drew his sword, and tested the edge with his finger. "That's kind of what I mean." He looked at Ed. "The war may be over in a matter of days."

Kibble agreed with a smile. "By the way, I stashed away about 100 more scanners. Let's give one or two to each plane. The enemy air force will come to an immediate end."

Lex joined in. "So, are we really thinking about staying in Britain? I mean, I think we should check out what's going on in America about now."

"Exactly." Kibble nodded to Lex. "This is a different time thread. What's happening in the Pacific? Maybe we can save Pearl Harbor from an attack."

Alexander turned his seat to see in the back. "We haven't had time to discuss much with Chad. Are you a historian? What do you think of all this?"

Chad chuckled. "I'm still wondering if this is all a dream! But really, I think the Brits can handle it from here. Let's see what we can do in the USA."

"You said it right." Lex weighed in on the conversation. "Don't forget. What we're really doing here is looking for a place to live."

The long trip back finally came to an end without further engagement. While the bombers landed on the runway, the C-2 descended straight down to the ground next to the office building. The crew disembarked and stood around waiting for Colonel Dunn.

Not long afterwards, the Colonel came bouncing spryly up to the office, pumping his fists in the air, as though he had personally just won the war.

"I don't know where you people are really from, but you are going to save all of our butts!" He reached the C-2 crew but didn't stop talking. "I'll tell you we need these scanners in the air, on land, and at sea! That's how we're going to win this blasted war fast!"

Strutting over to Alexander, he used his arms for emphasis. "You've got to get us hundreds of these scanners! Wherever they came from, go get us some more! We have to kick some Nazi butt while they're down! Don't let them try to steal some of these!"

Alexander smiled and nodded. "Yes Colonel, we'll get 500 of them for you by tomorrow. At that time, we will brief you on their use. But tonight, we'll need a place to stay."

"Done!" The Colonel agreed, pointing to the office. "Come in, I'll give you the key to a house here on base."

The two men stepped into the office, and Colonel Dunn opened a cupboard door with keys hanging on the inside. Grabbing one, he thrust it into Alexander's hand. "Get some rest, and I'll see you at 0800 hours."

Alexander laughed, grabbing the Colonel's hand for a shake. "We will see you then."

25

The key was labelled #17, and the house proved easy to find. It was a single house with a lawn and fenced back yard. Derek then went after the C-2 and landed it neatly in the backyard.

Lex supervised dinner, mixing food from the C-2 with canned food found in the kitchen cupboards. At the table, she was the first to open conversation. "I assume we'll be travelling to America tomorrow."

Everyone looked for Alexander to answer, which he did. "I'm sure the Colonel wants us to stay longer, but Derek and Ed will go back to 2030 tonight. They will go to the warehouse and load up 600 scanners. 500 will be given to the British, and we'll take the rest to America with us."

Ed continued the thought. "Remember the 8am briefing on how to use the scanners. I assume I'll be doing that."

"Sure." Kibble added. "After that we'll be taking off."

Lex shook her head. "He might try to detain us. He has strong persuasive powers."

Chad confidently chipped in. "I think at the end of the briefing, we should all jump in the C-2, and just take off. No bargaining or discussion. I mean, they'll have their scanners."

Lex nodded her approval. "Now that's an idea. Our work is done here. We have to move on."

Derek weighed in. "What part of America are we travelling to in 1940?"

Kibble chuckled. "That could be a quandary, but I suggest checking in at Pearl Harbor. If all is well, we'll do our old trick again. Materialize on the White House lawn."

Derek's surprised look turned to laughter. "Of course! That worked like a charm before!"

After dinner, Ed and Derek took their trip to 2030, materializing inside the warehouse. Loading up 600 scanners was uneventful, and almost too easily, they arrived back at the house.

That evening, Alexander had a good time relaxing, and eating popcorn for the first time. He did stand after the festivities and look around. "We have a big day tomorrow. I suggest we retire early."

Everyone followed suit, finding places to sleep. They were so tired, the morning seemed to come instantly.

At 0800, the C-2 and crew were at the airfield office. The scanners were being unloaded and piled next to the office door. By the time everyone arrived, the job was done.

Ed stood to speak to every pilot and co-pilot at the same time. Colonel Dunn stood at the forefront.

Ed began by holding up a scanner for all to see. "This is the most effective weapon in your military. It will not shoot down a plane, or kill a soldier, but it will jam any weapon, making it easy to shoot it down or blow it up."

He searched his audience to make sure they were paying attention. He then continued. "Each scanner has a scope to bring your target closer. When you pull the trigger, you will feel a vibration, which tells you that it's working. Once a weapon is scanned, it is ineffective until you change the setting to reverse and pull the trigger again. Once you scan every enemy plane in sight, everyone must shoot them down with your conventional weapons. One thing to remember is that your scanner will also jam the bombing mechanism, so the doors won't open to drop the bombs. Be very careful not to scan your own planes."

Ed opened his mouth to continue, but stood, frozen, and unable to speak. His eyes were fixed on the sky.

Suddenly Colonel Dunn yelled, "Enemy bombers! Grab a scanner and go!" Every Spitfire pilot reached down and ran to their planes. Thirty planes started down the runway. Kibble then barked an order. "Fire from the ground before our planes get up there!" He grabbed a scanner and looked skyward through the scope. Everyone got the message, firing at every bomber and fighter in the sky.

26

The C-2 crew worked feverishly to hit everything in the sky. After the Spitfires reached the enemy, it wouldn't be easy to tell them apart.

The targets of the bombing attack were unknown. Once scanned, each invading plane would be helpless. Finally, the last of the Luftwaffe had passed over, and the British fighters were up and after them. All was quiet.

"Let's go after them!" Alexander yelled. Within ten seconds the crew were all in their seats. The C-2 could go faster than any 1940's plane, and quickly caught up to the battle. No bombs had been dispensed yet.

"The Spitfires have scanners!" Kibble called out. "But we don't know if they know how to use them."

Ed butted in. "Just assume they haven't scanned anyone! We need to get everyone!" Scanning from their lofty position above the bomber group, they easily picked off enemy aircraft.

Lex happened to glance out the back window just in time to see an enemy fighter veer in behind them. Its guns opened fire instantly. She gasped as she pulled the scanner trigger, and just as quickly, the guns stopped. Suddenly the engine caught fire, and the plane bowed out on a downward trend. Then she saw the Spitfire behind it.

Looking around, it was apparent that the enemy was being shot down at a fast clip. The scanners had worked, and now the British fighters were now cherry picking.

Alexander soon checked below and was unable to identify any enemy aircraft. "I think we're done in Britain." He glanced at Derek. With raised eyebrows, Derek returned the glance. "Want to check on Pearl Harbor?"

Alexander didn't hesitate. "Yes, that's the next move."

Derek gained altitude to avoid coming in too low over Pearl Harbor. He then did calculations and programming.

Looking over his shoulder, he announced what he was doing. "We'll be flying over Pearl Harbor now." He hesitated, then pushed the button.

As they boomed into Pearl Harbor, Derek looked around. "By the way, this is December 6, 1941. We have time to talk to someone about the attack tomorrow morning at 8am."

Kibble's voice chimed in. "Best place to go would be Hickam Field. Not sure where that is."

Derek accessed the computer's library of information, and soon brought up a map. "Ok, it's not far away, so here we go." He brought the C-2 down to a lower altitude and buzzed off toward his destination. In a few minutes, Hickam Field came into view. He glided down and approached for a landing. "This looks like headquarters. We'll see."

As the aircraft touched down, several airmen came running out the front door.

27

Alexander opened his door and spoke over his shoulder. "Power down, Derek. Kibble and Ed, let's go."

Everyone else sat tight, while those three men stepped out, and faced the gathering crowd of airmen around the C-2.

Holding one arm up, Alexander looked sternly at the crowd. "We are here to see your commanding officer!" All the men looked toward the office door, where a tall, slender officer was emerging. Everyone made way for him, as he stepped confidently up to the three visitors.

Looking up at the C-2, his brow wrinkled, and he paused for a moment. "What is this? Who are you men?"

Kibble jumped at this question, thinking he was the most qualified to answer. "Can we speak with you in private? It's very important."

The commanding officer signaled to stop with his hand. "First of all, I'm Colonel Chase. I want to know who you are."

Kibble continued. "We are friends who have news that could save over 3,000 American lives tomorrow morning."

Colonel Chase froze momentarily, as he was opening his mouth to speak. He focused on Kibble before answering. "Let's step in here for a moment." Turning to his men, he issued an order. "Stay here and guard the aircraft. I'll be right back."

The Colonel motioned to his three strange visitors to follow. Through the headquarters door they went, all filing into the CO's office. Colonel Chase bore a look of confusion, as he sat at his desk. He shook his head, trying to figure out the men seated in front of him. He nervously rubbed the right side of his face, scrutinizing each of the men.

"Gentlemen, I need to know who you are before we go any further." He continued. "I have never seen an aircraft like yours. You're not dressed like normal people. What's going on?"

Kibble and Alexander exchanged glances, before Alexander spoke up.

"I'm just going to tell you straight out." He flashed a serious look at the Colonel. "We know what's going to happen here tomorrow morning at 8am."

The Colonel wrinkled his brow. "I haven't heard of anything unusual happening tomorrow." His eyes fastened on Alexander. "How would you know what's happening?"

"Colonel Chase," Alexander's voice carried the authority of a monarch. "We know because we've been to the future...and the past."

The Colonel's mouth dropped open.

Kibble took over. "You see, Colonel, we are time travelers. We are here to help you avoid a major disaster."

Silence ensued until Ed decided to join in the fray. "Colonel Chase, at 0800 tomorrow, the Japanese are going to attack Pearl Harbor. Three thousand people are going to die."

The Colonel shook his head. "Ok, gentlemen, it's tough to swallow this." He issued a fake laugh. "Look, if you want to convince me, you're going to have to take me to the future."

Kibble nodded. "That won't be a problem. Do you have a little time right now?"

"Yes." The answer was direct and matter of fact. "I've got to see if you guys are for real."

28

On his way into the C-2, Colonel Chase spoke once to his second in command. "I'll be back." He was given the co-pilot's seat for a good view.

Kibble spoke as he buckled in. "Derek, take us to the Japanese carriers prior to the attack, say 0700 on December 7."

Derek programmed and started the journey to the next day without saying a word. Colonel Chase was startled, grabbing both arms of his chair in desperation. But he didn't utter a word during the spinning and whirling periods.

Suddenly it was directly below them...the entire contingent. Four heavy carriers with 353 aircraft on deck. In all there were 30 ships and 35 submarines.

The Colonel sat speechless, but Alexander had not lost his speech. "Begin scanning now!" Everyone started silently shooting through the windows, except Derek. He used the C-2 scanner to disable planes, canons, and handguns. Men were scurrying about the ship decks trying to shoot down the C-2.

Derek moved on to all the carriers, then to the battleships and destroyers. Even the submarines had surfaced and were shooting hull mounted guns at them. But none lasted long enough to cause any damage.

Soon Alexander felt they had disabled the entire fleet. The C-2 silently glided around checking every ship and plane. Then he noticed that the planes were taking off anyway.

Colonel Chase appeared to panic. "We'd better get back right now and warn them!"

"No need to worry." Alexander quickly reassured the Colonel. "Their weapons have all been disabled. That includes bombs and missiles."

Kibble leaned forward. "Derek, let's go back now so they can dispatch planes and weapons against them."

Immediately Derek programmed and executed a return trip to Hickam field. Within minutes they were doing a vertical landing at headquarters. Colonel Chase literally jumped to the ground and ran through the door.

Within minutes, American P-40s took off, and headed for the Japanese coordinates. In all, about 200 fighters took to the air, and joined the force. With the Colonel back in his seat, the C-2 took off and followed the American defense force. The C-2's superior speed got them to the front in no time. Not far past the harbor, the two opposing groups collided.

It was only then that the Japanese realized their weapons didn't work. They were frantic, and it showed in their flight patterns. When they tried to shoot, or deploy bombs or missiles, the pilot was dead in the water. American pilots closed in and massacred the entire attack force. Every plane from the carriers was shot down.

After all was quiet, a group of B-17s showed up. It didn't take long for them to reach the carriers, and the rest of the armada. The subs disappeared, but all else was lost.

Colonel Chase shook his head, looking back at Alexander. "So, you people really are from the future."

Alexander nodded. "All except me. I'm from the past."

The Colonel appeared confused and posed another question. "Are you telling me that their attack on Pearl Harbor the first time was successful?" Kibble nodded. "They sank all of your ships and destroyed most of your planes. Like I said, over 3'000 Americans died."

Colonel Chase smiled. "Well, I have you to thank. I'll be ending my career in a blaze of glory instead of shameful defeat."

Kibble reached up and patted the Colonel's shoulder. "We're also saving more lives than you think. World war 2 cost 75 million lives. It's amazing to prevent most of those people from dying."

29

The time travelers met to discuss their nest course of action. The government had put them up in a hotel in Honolulu, which was the meeting location.

Alexander, who still carried his sword, pulled it out and sat it on the coffee table. "Folks, we are here to talk about our next move." He looked at the five people around him. "If you remember, our main goal was to find a safe and pleasant place to live."

He thumbed the sword handle before continuing. "I think this is a great time to check the future. We may find what we're looking for."

"I'll put in my two cents worth." Lex joined in, sitting casually with her ankles crossed, and her arms over the sides of the chair. "I know we stopped the war, and I guess we're going to be heroes again. But I don't think I would like living in the 1940s." She looked around. "Does anybody know what we should do now?" She asked, sounding as though she already knew the answer.

After a short silence, Derek spoke. "Well, it's a no-brainer that when we go to the future, they will remember us."

"But what year do we choose?" Kibble posed.

Ed chipped in. "Far enough to be part of the history books."

"Well," Alexander picked up his sword, and ran his finger along the blade. "The year 2028 worked last time."

Chad piped up. "That's about 83 years into the future. Should be enough time to check the progress of society."

"Yes, I think that's perfect." Ed jumped in again. "We should get back to our own time in history in order to benefit from our own scientific research."

Alexander picked up his sword and slipped it snuggly into its sheath. "It looks like we have a consensus." He smiled. "We go to 2028."

The time travelers were within walking distance of Hickam field, where the C-2 was kept. On the way, they discussed a course of action to follow.

They were not about to openly load up and take off for fear of being detained. So, the group went to a nearby park, while Derek climbed a fence near the C-2, and casually boarded, and flew straight up. He then dropped by the park.

With everyone in their seats, he quickly gained altitude, and stopped at one mile high.

Alexander then made an announcement. "Before we go to 2028, I would like to make a suggestion. Since we don't really know what we will find, let's just observe a little, and then decide."

Kibble took the floor. "I agree, and I think we should go to Washington DC first. Hot the White House."

Ed spoke up. "Everyone, have your scanners ready for anything."

30

Derek programmed the trip to DC in 2028. With all passengers ready, they shot ahead 86 years. Suddenly they were high in the air above the nation's capital. Derek didn't hesitate to buzz to a lower altitude.

Everyone noticed that the terrain looked familiar. "Hmm, this is very strange." Alexander thought out loud. "I did a lot of travelling across the country when I ruled for two years." His brow wrinkled. "This looks like it did then."

Kibble spoke up. "Well, it is the same year you started." He paused. "But otherwise, I don't understand the connection."

Lex came up with an idea. "I suggest we go to the white house and see if we get any more clues."

Everyone nodded in agreement. Derek slipped into high speed for a few seconds to get there. Looking down, the time travelers were shocked. There was no white house!

"Oh, man!" Alexander exclaimed, while nervously rubbing the back of his neck. "If I didn't know better, I'd say this is the very time thread that we first arrived in."

Derek accelerated as he spoke. "Let's head to the capital building, shall we?"

Alexander nodded, and the C-2 buzzed along toward what would be the capital building. Lex was the first to exclaim. "It's there, the very same building!"

The wheels again turned in Alexander's head, but no conclusions were drawn. "Go ahead and set it down on the lawn." He ordered. "We're going to find out just what's going on."

Lex interjected. "The Kingdom was a whole different country that included Canada and Mexico." She shook her head. "We are supposed to be in the United States."

The C-2 coasted softly down, landing gently on the lawn. "Look," Kibble remarked, "the passersby are not staring at us. It's like they are accustomed to us landing here, just like in the United American Republics."

Alexander opened the door. "Kibble, Ed, let's go. We'll be back soon." He called over his shoulder.

The three men gathered, and strolled together to the sidewalk, and up to the building. Looking at one another, they opened the door, and stepped in.

Everyone who passed by them gave greetings, mentioning "Emperor", or "Professor Kibble", as he preferred to be called. The men experienced a strange and nostalgic feeling, like they had just stepped into yesterday.

They headed up to the 5th floor, and as the door opened, saw the emperor's office. The guards stood at attention while they passed. All was as it used to be.

Approaching his office door, Alexander looked at Kibble and Ed. "I'll go in first." He spoke this as he opened the door. The three steps to where he could see around the corner, took forever. Stepping around the corner Alexander scanned the room. It was empty. His heart skipped a beat, as he turned around and motioned for his friends to come in.

The three men met in the middle of the office. No one spoke until Alexander broke for the phone on a hunch. He picked it up and spoke. "Sally."

A voice came from the phone, "Yes, sir."

Alexander thought fast. "Have you seen Professor Kibble?"

The answer came. "Why, no, sir. All of you have been gone for two weeks. We didn't know where you went."

"Thank you." He reassured her. "We're back now."

As he hung up the phone, he saw the expressions on Ed's and Kibble's faces.

As they stood there, all three men were totally confused, but happy at the same time. They were home.

31

As the three overjoyed men stood in the emperor's office, Alexander had another spontaneous idea. He quickly picked up the phone again, and called his leading military man, General Bradford. The surprised general greeted the emperor. Alexander tried to explain their absence. "We were on a classified mission, but just returned. I need an update on the weapons shutdown system."

There was a short silence, but General Bradford's answer came. "Yes, sir. The system is working perfectly in every field of operation."

"Very good." Alexander returned. "Now I want efforts doubled to search out any real danger there."

"Absolutely." The General answered. "We'll get right on it, in every part of the world."

"Thank you. That will be all." Alexander softly put the phone down. He looked at Kibble and Ed. "It's possible that our counter selves will return any time."

Kibble's look was one of questioning. "But why the secrecy of our absence? It just doesn't make any sense."

"No, it doesn't." Ed agreed. "But it could just be one of the mysteries of time travel. We may be back where we're supposed to be."

Alexander nodded. "Why don't you gentlemen go tell the rest of our crew to just go home as they normally would. And to let me know if anyone runs into their counter selves. I'll be in the office for a while."

Kibble and Ed nodded, and moved toward the door. Kibble remarked over his shoulder.

"We'll let you know of anything strange at all happening."

As they stepped onto the sidewalk, the two messengers saw a few friends gathered around the C-2. All were chatting as though time had stood still. The crew knew it hadn't, but they weren't about to let on to anyone.

Kibble and Ed delivered the message and were on their way to find quarters for Chad. Derek and Lex were meandering toward their respective homes, when something strange happened.

The figure of a man running caught their eyes. He was heading directly toward them. Suddenly Lex's jaw dropped, and she froze in her tracks. It was her husband, James Jacobs, who slowed down and greeted everyone. He walked straight to Lex and embraced her.

She clung to him for a long time. The other crew members just stood around in wonderment. All had thought Reverend Jacobs to be either dead or gone forever.

When Lex regained composure, she looked into his eyes, and asked the question she'd been wanting to ask him for so long. "Where have you been for the last two years?"

James was taken back, raising his eyebrows with a look of confusion. His answer came as he placed one arm around her while glancing at Derek Kibble, and Ed. "Honey, you folks have only been gone for two weeks."

Everyone was speechless for a moment. Kibble broke the silence. "Well, you have been gone from us for two years." He paused for a moment. "Do you remember time travelling, and not coming back?" James scratched his head, then he shook it. "That's beyond me. I don't recall it. What have you folks been doing for two years?"

Lex touched his lips with her finger. "It's going to take some time to explain that." James appeared even more confused but came through with a smile and a kiss for Lex. "We are going to have lots of time." Looking around, he smiled again. "Shall we all go home, then?"

Lex grinned. "That's where we're going." She grabbed his arm, and they left together.

32

The next day the group met in Alexander's office to try and make sense out of recent events. Alexander opened by opening the floor. "I'd like to listen to any ideas about what's going on, and what we should do at this point."

James spoke up. "It might help you to hear it from my perspective. As I've said, to all of us, all of you have been gone only two weeks."

Kibble jumped in. "Did we say where we were going, and why?"

James smiled and shook his head. "That's the strange thing about all this. You said nothing, and you suddenly just disappeared."

Heads were shaking all around. "I can't make sense out of this." Ed weighed in. "I think we should just chalk this one up to the mysteries of time travel."

Lex, still her brash self, laid it on the line for everyone. "We have to stop worrying about this. Whatever happened, happened; and we just need to focus on the here and now. We're here now, so what should we do next?"

Alexander chuckled and held up his hand. "Yes, that's why we had this meeting in the first place. To talk about what comes next." He stood up and did a slow pace, deep in thought. He stopped, and pulled his sword half- way out, then slammed it back in.

"Ok this is the plan." He stepped back and sat down again. "We are going to live as though we've come back, and this is still our home."

A lively applause with cheers ripped through the room. Derek then added a serious thought. "The most important thing to focus on right now would be the weapons shutdown system. We don't want the same thing to happen again."

"Exactly!" Kibble vigorously agreed. "Alexander talked about this already. We've got to ensure the safety of the world."

Alexander nodded. "Kibble and Ed know that I've already spoken to my head General about this. So, you two will go back to your labs, unless I need you. Derek back to time travel studies and aviation. James, I assume you still have your church for you and Lex to attend to." An enthusiastic nod came from James, with smiles from Lex.

"Great!" Alexander pumped a fist in the air. "The last order of business today is Chad." His gaze caught Chad, who was sitting next to him with folded hands, and a pleasant demeanor.

"Chad, I know you were a city mayor. My question to you is, do you want to stay in politics?"

A swift nod came from Chad. "Absolutely." Was his short, emphatic answer.

"That will be arranged." Alexander leaned back in his chair. "Second question is, do you want to be a member of this time travel group?"

Chad wasted no time answering. "Yes, sir. This is an amazing group. I believe I can contribute."

Alexander cracked a smile and gestured to the other members. "Welcome, then!" Applause came from all around the table.

Alexander held up one arm. "If there's nothing more to discuss at this time, I'm going to be doing a lot of travelling for a while to be sure the defense system is up to par. Chad, we'll get you started right away. Kibble will be in charge while I'm gone."

A brief pause. "Thank you all!" The group dispersed, with everyone thankful for a second chance at saving the beautiful utopia they had stumbled upon for the second time.

33

Alexander went to every weapons shutdown stronghold in the world and ran into a few surprises. The natives in every country were friendly, obliging, and helpful to him, who was supposed to be their enemy. He arrived back home scratching his head, wondering why the difference between now and his former experience.

At a meeting in his office with Kibble and Ed, he expressed his bewilderment. "This is nothing like before. We had to set up defenses all over. Now everyone acts like we're on the same side!"

Kibble fiddled with his mustache before replying. "Do you know what this sounds like to me? We're in a parallel time thread! Don't know how we got here, but it's an almost identical world. Obviously, there are differences, some of which are big."

Ed was amazed. "Wow! This is very fortunate for us. Everything seems to be coming up roses." He rubbed his chin. "But I would caution against being lax about anything. Keep our guard up, keep the defenses up, and don't let anyone get information on the shutdown system. Even citizens of this country. It should be on a need-to-know basis."

Alexander nodded. "That's how I've been approaching it so far. That's a good idea, and gentlemen...let's keep researching for improvements in the system."

As the meeting was adjourned, the door swung open after a brief knock, and around the corner burst Derek. He seemed out of breath. "Good, you're here! Something's very wrong with the future. In one year, we are going to become a police state! Don't yet know who will be in power, but it won't be us!"

The three men stared in disbelief. Finally, Alexander pulled out a chair. "Please sit down."

Derek brushed the back of his arm over his forehead, and sat down, taking a deep breath and exhaling.

"Just start from the beginning." Alexander pulled up a chair and sat in front of him. Kibble and Ed followed suit.

"I was just doing my normal routine." Derek began. "I jumped ahead a few months at a time to check the stability of the future. When I got to one year, everything was different. There was a lot of military presence, and road-blocks on the streets." He paused for a moment. "Oh, and there were a lot of people walking around in middle eastern garb...tunics and robes."

The men exchanged glances. Alexander frowned. "Did you discover exactly when the overthrow took place?"

"Yes." Derek confidently answered. "On June 14 everything around this building looked normal. On June 15 it all changed. Soldiers, different flag, I didn't recognize it. A lot of gunfire heard all over."

Alexander sat up in his chair and looked around. "Alright, this is what we will do. Tomorrow morning, Derek, Kibble, and Chad will go back there to find out some more details. Then come back and report to me. Definitely take scanners with you."

"Ed, of course, we need you here doing more fine tuning on the shutdown system." He looked at Ed. "This is high priority. We need to keep an upper hand." Ed nodded.

Kibble wagged his head at Alexander. "And everything was looking so good."

The next morning, Kibble, Derek, and Chad met at the C-2 on the airfield. They huddled outside for a brief confab. "We're going to collect information." Kibble opened. "It's just a reconnaissance mission, and a return trip. We will all keep our scanners handy."

"Are we going to remain airborne?" Chad queried.

"That is our goal." Came the answer. "Let's hope we don't have to land."

Derek lightly gripped Kibble's arm. "I assume we'll start out with high altitude."

Kibble nodded. "Certainly. So, let's go."

The men loaded, buckled in, and buzzed upward. At 1,000 feet, Derek stopped. "Ok," Kibble began, "go to June 14, and we'll work our way to the 15th. Let's see exactly what it was, and when the attack was made."

While Derek did the programming, Kibble and Chad secured their scanners in hand.

34

Momentarily, the C-2 popped into June 14, nearly a year into the future. So far everything looked normal, so Derek cruised in the direction of the Capitol building. Within a few minutes they arrived, with all still appearing normal.

"Go forward two hours now." Kibble sounded calm.

The C-2 warped ahead two hours, and all was unchanged.

Kibble gave the order two more times to go ahead two hours, and nothing was happening. On the fifth time they jumped ahead, Chad instantly noticed a man below them in a hazmat suit. He had two tanks on his back, one with a hose to his hand carrying a spray gun. He was walking toward the Capitol building.

"Look down there! He shouted." Kibble almost jumped out of his seat.

"That could be chemical weapons! Scan it quick!" All three of the men aimed and blasted at the same time. Derek flew lower as the man looked up. He threw off the tanks and started running. Derek did not give chase but floated straight down and landed. He looked at a gauge on the panel. "Nothing's been released into the air! We can secure that!"

"I'll get it!" Kibble shouted as he opened his door. He stepped over and gathered it up carefully, opening an exterior compartment in the C-2, and gently laying the tanks in it.

As he climbed back into his seat, Derek noticed a large group of aircraft coming in toward them. He quickly gained altitude, and soon had a better view. "Looks like big transport planes." Chad offered his assessment. Kibble agreed. "That would mean they're carrying troops. Let's get a better look at them."

Derek flew toward them. As they drew nearer, they suddenly started firing at the C-2. Kibble jumped into action. "Fire scanners!" All three men scanned for all they were worth. After a couple minutes they stopped. No more gunfire came from the oncoming aircraft. The whole group did a 180 and went back to where they came from.

"That's enough." Kibble sounded satisfied. "Let's go to the capitol building and see who we find. Now maybe they can stop this attack."

Landing on the front lawn, all three men got out and headed in. On the top floor, Kibble knocked on the Emperor's office, and opened the door. As he walked into the room, he felt a strange vibe, like something was out of sync. Turning the corner, he then knew what it was. In a chair next to Alexander, was a blurry figure of a man...himself.

Kibble froze, but Alexander stood up and turned a knob on the wall. Kibble saw the blurry view of himself clear up, and he was left staring at his future self. The Kibble at the desk then spoke. "I guess you haven't seen my invention. It clears up distortion that is sometimes encountered by meeting your counterpart."

By this time, Derek and Chad stood next to Kibble, looking on with interest. Kibble bypassed the pleasantries, going straight to the point. "We are from another time thread, one year in the past, to warn you of danger occurring as we speak."

Alexander and the older Kibble looked at one-another and expressed concern. "What's going on?" Alexander inquired.

"We just stopped a chemical weapons attack on this building." Kibble began. "And we scanned ten troop planes heading this way to take over the capitol. I don't know what other places are under attack at this point."

Alexander held up one hand. "If there are any, I'll be hearing about them immediately. Thanks for the warning."

Kibble nodded but communicated one last detail. "The reason we are here, is because Derek just checked a year in advance, which is now, and found a police state. We have to beat this thing today, or it will be the end of your country."

Alexander smiled. "We are indebted to you, and we will handle this situation right now."

"Ok," Kibble replied. "We wish you good luck, and we will be checking on the future." Kibble turned and walked out, followed by Derek and Chad.

35

Once they were seated in the C-2, Derek spoke. "Right now, we should check ahead a day to see if we fixed it or not."

"Exactly right." Kibble agreed. "Then we can report to Alexander."

Derek flew the aircraft to 1000 feet. Then he poked a few keys, and they were on their way to tomorrow. When the pop came, they eagerly looked down, and saw nothing unusual.

Derek clapped his hands. "Yes! We did it!"

Kibble smiled. "Cause for celebration! Let's go home and do it."

"Well," Chad chipped in, "we know Alexander's going to be happy."

In a few minutes, they were knocking on and opening Alexander's door. Trooping around the corner, they found him at his computer studying. But he stood up in anticipation of Kibble's report.

Kibble looked at him and gave the thumbs up sign with a grin. "We fixed it! Found a guy trying to blast the capital building with chemical weapons. We then disabled ten transport planes heading our way. We also talked with our counterparts in the office. They were unaware but said they would get right on it."

"We also checked tomorrow, and it looked clear." Derek added.

Alexander slapped his chair in pure glee. "That simplifies things quite a bit!" He eyed the three men standing in front of him. "I'm going to tell General Bradford to find out which mid-eastern group did this and put the screws to them!" He smiled. "You gentlemen did a great job. Why don't you take the rest of the day off?"

Kibble, Derek, and Chad looked at each other in surprise, then laughed as they headed for the door. "Thanks a lot." Kibble replied. "You sure there's nothing else pressing today?"

"Don't see a thing." Alexander shook his head. "In fact, I might go home and take a nap. It's been pretty hot and heavy for all of us the last year. We need a break."

Kibble laughed. "I'll drink to that."

The two leaders walked out together to get some R&R.

Two weeks later all was still peace and tranquility, with no problems in sight. The time travelers knew that when things quiet down, they needed to take advantage of it for some real down time.

One month later, they were having a time traveler meeting in Alexander's office. "Things are going well all around." Alexander opened the meeting. "We are just finding out that our efforts with WW2 and Chiang Kai-shek have produced good results for the world and for us." He remained standing while the others sat at the table. Reaching for his sword, he pulled it out and ran his finger along the blade. He spun the sword in mid-air, and it flipped around faster than the eye could see, as the blade found its way into its sheath before anyone realized what was happening.

Eyes bugged out, and he continued as if nothing had transpired. "We have discovered who was responsible for the recent attempted chemical attack, and we have put a lid on that. The obvious question is now…what is next?"

He looked around, as if seeking an answer.

It was Lex who ultimately came up with an answer. "I suggest that nothing is wrong, and so we don't need to fix anything. Maybe that would mean that…well, nothing is next."

Laughter rippled across the table, and Alexander couldn't hold back a grin. "And you have my word, you won't be called unless it is a real emergency."

Chad raised his hand as he spoke. "Excuse my ignorance, since I'm new here. But do you now have an effective one world government?"

Alexander responded immediately. I don't see it as that really. The countries of the world can have independence, as long as they follow the rules we have set up. We have seen what happens when they don't…mass mayhem and death." Alexander gazed at the floor for a moment, his right hand resting on his sword. "We are not tyrants here. We only want peace and cooperation from everyone. I think it's worth it to rule with a strong hand, if that can be the result of it."

After a brief applause, Ed brought up a related topic. "I thought you and everyone here should know that I've had a breakthrough in my research of the weapons shutdown system. Using satellites has provided some great results. For example, I can now instantly see all the weapons in every country. I can also differentiate between our own weapons and foreign weapons. I can immediately shut down all unregistered weapons in an entire country."

"That is outstanding!" Alexander flashed a victory sign with his arms. "You know who to talk to about that. Will you see that this new system is implemented right away?"

"Absolutely." Ed nodded.

Alexander opened the floor again. "Are there any other new developments with research or otherwise?"

Derek responded. "This is new, but I know it's going to work. "I will be able to program the C-2's time travel system to transport us from one place to another at the touch of a key. If we're in China, and are under attack, I can instantly get us out of there. And if I don't preprogram a destination, it will default to the last location of the C-2. No more spinning and getting dizzy."

Alexander gave a shrug sign with his shoulders and arms. "This is fantastic news, in terms of our safety when out on surveillance trips. It will increase our power and security big time!"

36

The whole crew was greatly encouraged by the turn of events, and the new developments in research. They all enjoyed a season of peace and prosperity. This was very helpful, because it prepared them for their next challenge.

It had been apparent to Lex and James that something was wrong when she arrived home after a two-year absence, and to him it was only two weeks. But this didn't cause any relationship problems. The couple got along just as they always had and were very happy.

And the same type of experience had been going on in the lives of the rest of the time travelers, except Chad, the newcomer. When the group arrived, James had told them that they had only been gone for two weeks, and that he himself hadn't gone on the trip because of an illness. When they arrived, it was natural for James to think they were the very ones who had left two weeks ago. When that was discovered to be wrong, everyone just accepted each other anyway, in the absence of the group that actually belonged in this time thread.

One morning, everyone received a call to an urgent meeting in Alexander's office. As they sat at the big table, Alexander remained standing, appearing nervous, as though something had gone wrong. He gripped his sword handle, which was a sign that all was not well.

He started with an announcement. "There is no way to break this news to you gently. I have to just tell you. In ten minutes, all of our counterparts will arrive. That's why you are sitting on one side of the table." He pulled his sword halfway out, and then shoved it back in with some force. "These are the folks that really belong here, I'm sorry to say."

James and Lex looked at each other, and James took her hand in a gesture of love and reassurance. Alexander bore an expression of sympathy as he witnessed this. "Lex, I know your counterpart who belongs here is coming to replace you. However, I want to tell you that we think we can find James' counterpart. The one who actually belongs with us." He looked down while pacing aimlessly for a few feet. "This won't take all the pain away, but it will help."

Lex buried her face in one hand, while still gripping James' hand with the other. Her head wagged lightly, as tears escaped through her fingers. James put his arm around her trying to reassure her. This was a crazy and painful episode that could only happen with time travel.

All was silent for a moment, and then came a knock at the door. It opened immediately, and in filed the other group...Alexander, Kibble, Derek, Ed, and Lex. The fuzzy buzz that sometimes occurred from counterparts meeting, suddenly began. Kibble quickly stood and reached over to press the button on the wall. He had recently invented this, which was inspired by another counterpart of himself. All faces became clear, as the group walked around to the other side of the table and remained standing.

The two Alexanders shook each other's hand in a gesture of cooperation and friendship. The one who just arrived then spoke to everyone. "I know that our arrival causes a great upheaval in your lives." He looked at Lex and James seated at the table. Then standing, Lex bit her lower lip, and turned away from the strange and unnatural sight of seeing her husband with another woman...her own counterpart.

Alexander continued. "I have left information with your leader that may take you all to your rightful home in another time thread." His arm gestured to the other Alexander. "I really think it's better for us not to tarry long. You all can go home and collect the things you need." He gripped his sword in frustration. "Again, I'm very sorry to cause this traumatic event."

Everyone made eye contact with their counterparts, nervously. The group that was seated then stood and started for the door...Alexander in the lead. Quietly, they exited the room, leaving their beautiful utopia behind. Lex and James squeezed hands one last time, as James fell out of line and stepped over to the other Lex. She stared at him for one awkward moment, then embraced him.

37

Everyone went home just to gather their things, and report in 30 minutes at the C-2, which was in the airfield. Before meeting time, everyone had arrived, standing around by the C-2.

Alexander called a group huddle before leaving. "This is our agenda. My counterpart got this information from his Derek. It's coordinates for a time thread that they visited. All of the time travel group had been gone for a couple of years." He looked at Lex. "Except James. They didn't see James but were told he was involved in a church function, so he wasn't around."

Lex looked encouraged. "That sounds promising...like he's actually there."

Alexander nodded and smiled.

"And yes, the place where they found his location was this city's counterpart...Castle City." He placed his hand on Lex's shoulder. "I believe he's the one who really belongs with us."

Alexander handed Derek the paper with the coordinates on it, and then gave the thumbs up. "OK, let's go!" Everyone piled into the C-2, and it took Derek just a moment to program the trip to a specific time thread.

Then they all found out that Derek was right when he said he had perfected the lag, fuzziness, and dizziness during time travel sequences. One second, they were waiting, and the next they had suddenly transported instantly to their destination.

"Wow!" Kibble exclaimed. "That's a fine piece of research. A smooth transition."

As they looked out the windows, they noticed only a few differences from the Castle City they just left. But they were hardly worth mentioning. The differences only showed that, indeed they were two separate cities, and were two separate time threads.

Derek spoke up. "Maybe we haven't seen the leaders because we are the true leaders here. That means this really is our home!"

"Yes!" Lex pumped her arm. "All we have to do is find James!"

Derek glanced at Alexander, who gave the nod, and he quickly engaged the C-2, which flew up and out toward James' residence.

"After the nuclear destruction," Lex spoke as she leaned forward in her seat. "they may not have rebuilt everything the same way. Our house may not even be there."

"True." Alexander agreed. "We'll see if it is and go from there."

In two minutes, they arrived at the right spot, but no house was in sight. Lex sighed. "What day is this?"

"Uh, Wednesday." Derek quickly replied.

"Then he could be in a meeting at the church." She announced. "We should go there next."

"And is the church in the same place?" He asked the obvious question. He got no answer, so he sped on to where the church used to be. Within another two minutes, there was the answer. "There it is!" He excitedly shouted.

Lex was thrilled as she unbuckled her seat belt. "Land and let me go look for a minute!" She exuberantly commanded Derek. Not even Alexander could refuse her now.

The craft landed on the lawn softly and powered down. Lex shoved the door open and jumped out. She bolted across the lawn and went through the front door, encouraged by a lot of cars in the parking lot.

The other time travelers looked at each other and got out to follow her. Lex was in the church foyer and barged through the doors of the sanctuary. She found the pews full of people, who all looked up and stared at her.

Lex didn't care about anything but finding James. Her eyes trailed ahead to the front of the church. On the podium, behind the pulpit, was a man in a dark suit. She stopped and stared for a moment to be sure. She then raced down the aisle, up the stairs, and behind the pulpit. She smiled big, as she grabbed a wide-eyed, confused James Jacobs, and kissed him in front of a jam-packed church.

Cheers and applause came from everywhere, and didn't stop for several minutes, as James, now smiling, held onto his long-lost wife. Obviously, it was something his congregation knew history about.

38

The other time travelers opened the sanctuary doors, and peeked in, admiring the scene. Soon they were recognized, and the congregation started chanting Alexander's name. The voices grew louder, until he gave in and waved as he walked up to the pulpit.

Alexander shook hands with James and stepped up to the microphone.

"This was definitely not planned, but we found our way back here, mostly by accident, and when we heard James was here, Lex was not to be denied. So, here we are!"

The crowd cheered and clapped. Several people shouted, "We still need you! This is your country!"

As parting words, Alexander looked all around the big church. "I hope we can stay. We certainly would love to!"

With that, he walked down the stairs toward the exit. Everyone except Lex followed him. She sat down on the front row and crossed her legs. An overjoyed Reverend James Jacobs finished up his prayer meeting.

After the meeting, when all the well-wishers had gone home, James sat down next to his wife whom he thought he would never see again. Turning to face her, he grasped her hand and shook his head in

unbelief. "I never thought. I was afraid we wouldn't meet again. It's been two years!"

Lex started laughing. "I just spent three months with your counterpart, whom I hadn't seen for two years. But he had been away from me for two weeks!" She looked at James. "Something has gone terribly wrong here. But I think we just fixed our end of it!"

James drew close. "Let's keep it that way." He smiled and kissed.

The rest of the time travelers sat in the C-2 hashing out a plan of action.

Ed opened the conversation since no one else was doing much talking. "There's something very important we need to keep in mind here." He made eye contact with everyone. "I believe this is our original time thread. If that's true, then there was nuclear destruction here. Most of the other threads had nukes too, but I think this was the only thread with no leaders afterward, and I mean us as leaders."

He looked again to see if everyone was paying attention. "That means this country has been weak for the last two years. Infiltrated with enemy troops. They have essentially taken over."

Kibble filled in the last part. "Of course, that means we will have a real challenge to steady the ship. It's going to be tough to regain what we've lost."

Alexander joined in the train of thought. "If they haven't captured the weapons shutdown system, we have a good chance."

"Even if they have," Ed added, "I've made some significant progress on the technology. I think we can still beat them."

Alexander began nodding. "We have a big obstacle to overcome, but we are up to the challenge. Let's head to the Capitol building and get started."

39

The men in the C-2 buzzed off toward Castle City. Alexander, Kibble, Ed, Derek, and Chad did not know what would greet them when they reached the Capitol building.

Ed commented as they approached their destination. "Once we get there, I will need a little time to install the new system… maybe an hour."

Kibble nodded. "We will cover for you while you're working." He turned to a drawer in the panel and pulled out five pistols. "These are stun guns set on maximum, which means they'll be out for quite a while."

Ed continued. "Let's try the scanners first. If they work, we won't need to stun anyone."

As they descended next to the building, several things were obviously wrong. First, their flag was down, and in its place was one that was unrecognizable. It seemed to be a conglomeration of Arab states that were overlaid with something resembling a swastika. Alexander's voice sounded intense. "We are going to have to depend on our new technology. There's only one way to do this." He looked around as Derek landed on the lawn. "We're going in."

Ed grabbed his tool case, and quickly unloaded with the crew. Alexander led the way, and the men casually strolled to the sidewalk, and up to the doors. They were getting strange looks from passersby and officials on site. Some shady looking characters started following them.

Alexander ducked into the stairway, trailed by the others. Everything inside looked like a military operation. No familiar faces were seen.

At the 5th and final floor, he peeked cautiously through the small window on the door. Two soldiers, in full combat gear, guarded the elevator. He held one finger to his mouth signaling silence, then pulled out his scanner. Aiming it through the window, he pulled the tripper, targeting each man's weapon. He spoke softly. "Stun guns next." He pulled his out, and the others followed suit.

Alexander casually opened the door, went through, and started speaking to the guards. They were alarmed and began to aim their rifles at him. He was ready. He swiftly drew his sword and nailed each man over the head with the handle. He motioned for the others to follow. They quickly jogged to the head office and opened the door carefully. As he lightly stepped around the corner, Kibble was right behind him.

Immediately they saw three men in the room dressed in class A military uniforms. They all grabbed for their pistols, but Kibble and Alexander were ahead of the game. Alexander took out the first one with his sword, while Kibble used the stun gun to mow down the other two in quick fashion.

Alexander grabbed the phone and dialed the number of his most trustworthy general, even though two years had gone by. To his surprise, general Harrington answered.

"Sam, this is Alexander. Can you talk?" The answer came from a shocked Sam Harrington. "I had no idea what happened to you! But don't say anything on the phone."

"Ok, listen. This is a Code 6. And I know you remember Code 6. We need help now. Are you at the same address?"

"Yes, sir, and the coast is clear now."

Alexander had second thoughts. "Look, we've taken over my office. We'll need help right away. See what you can do!"

"Will do, Alexander. You can count on me."

Alexander hung up and checked around. "We should have help on the way. He knows Code 6 is an active military coup, and he knows how to get reinforcements and weapons." Ed spoke up. "Alexander, I think it would be much better for us to get out of here for the time being. Just too many of them, and not enough of us."

Kibble nodded. "I agree. We can do this, but we need a little more organization."

Alexander delivered a quick nod. "Ok let's go find Sam." He made a fast exit out the door, and toward the stairwell.

40

The group made a swift beeline to the stairs and descended silently. At every level they checked the window. On the first floor, Alexander looked through the glass, and all seemed to be semi-normal. He opened the door and walked out acting relaxed, to ward off undue attention. His steps were speedy and sure. The men unwaveringly followed his every move. At the outside door he didn't hesitate but marched directly to the C-2.

At this point, a few military and Arab-garbed types, eyed them and walked curiously toward their aircraft.

"Take us out of here!" He barked, as everyone loaded up double time.

Derek was lifting off in a matter of seconds and elevated straight up at full speed. Ed and Kibble scanned everyone in sight to ensure the C-2 wouldn't be attacked.

At 3,000 feet, Derek hovered, and waited for further orders.

"Here's what we'll do." Alexander looked at Derek. "Program a time travel sequence to Sam's house just after we hung up the phone…about 20 minutes ago. I know he's got a big back yard. Set us down right there." He handed Derek a piece of paper with Sam's address written on it.

Derek punched it in. Alexander gave him the thumbs up. "Let's go."

Derek hit the enter key, and it took three seconds to send the aircraft and crew to their exact destination.

Alexander jumped out and ran into the house. Sam was still standing by the phone after hanging up. He had a puzzled look on his face.

"It was too dangerous to stay there." Alexander explained. "But Sam, we have better technology now. With a little help, we can send these thugs on their way."

Sam nodded and looked outside. "Tell them to come in for coffee. Sit down."

In five minutes, everyone was sitting around the table sipping coffee. Sam spoke first. "If I seem surprised to you, it's because we thought you were dead." He grinned. "It's great to see you alive!" Alexander half smiled. "Well, it's good to be alive." He sipped his coffee.

"So, what's the verdict? Can we get any underground support?"

"Of course." Sam replied. "But frankly, I think we could get the dirty work done quickly if we just do it like a real coup is supposed to be done. Just grab the power and send them packing."

Alexander squeezed his cup in thought. "Do we have any special ops units still active?"

Sam winced. "Sorry. I can get some patriots together, but basically, the only special ops units will be us…you and me."

"Ok." Alexander looked at Sam. "You and your men take over the airport, while we secure the capitol building."

He leaned back and grabbed his sword handle, pulling it out and thrusting it back in. "Tell me when you're ready. We have to coordinate it at the same time."

41

The men stayed at Sam's that night to coordinate with him in the morning. Sam made a few phone calls that morning to organize patriots for a military coup. It didn't take long, especially when they heard that Alexander was back.

Alexander shared some scanners out of the C-2 with Sam. In return, Sam took the group to his secret weapons location, and shared with them.

Finally, the entire force of underground fighters got together to discuss plans. Mostly it was just coordinating times. Sam didn't share with Alexander many details of operation, and neither did Alexander share much. Neither man really knew much of how they were going to accomplish this. It was going to be a work in progress, execute as you go type of operation.

Everyone was now equipped with formidable firearms, as well as smoke bombs, grenades, and plenty of ammo. Chad was given a rocket propelled grenade launcher.

At noon the groups separated and agreed to keep in contact with one another. The time travelers loaded into the C-2, with plans to either scan or blast their way into the building. This did not appeal to Alexander, and he appeared to be deep in thought.

When everyone loaded in, he stood for a last-minute consultation. He sounded resolute as he spoke. "We may well end up fighting on the ground, but we are going to carry out this campaign in the air as long as possible."

He pointed to the windows all around the aircraft. "Use the scanners all you can. They are effective." He jiggled his sword in and out for a few seconds. "It's true they may have scanners themselves, but it's also true that ours are more effective, and can null the effect of their scanners."

He looked toward the pilot's chair. "Derek let's just fly all over and knock out as many guns with the scanners as we can. That is our advantage and will be how we're going to win this thing."

Alexander sat down and strapped in, as Derek started the engine and took off. The sleek, nimble C-2 glided around, and the men began seeing all the military equipment on the ground. Anywhere they spotted a weapon, it was immediately scanned by all. They encountered missiles, cannons, SAMs, flak

guns, tanks, and much more spread out all over the urban areas. Several times they saw men on the ground with scanners pointed at them. But the C-2 just scanned the scanners, disabling them.

Ed laughed every time, offering a scornful reproach. "Those poor devils don't know that they can't touch my anti-scanning technology."

He had installed this new technology in the C-2 and all hand scanners.

Before long there were jet fighters coming after them. This was tricky, because they couldn't see them coming in the distance, so had to rely on the instrument panel detection instruments. They could then point their scanners in the right direction before the enemy deployed missiles at them. But they were doing it, and every plane in the air was decommissioned. Derek even shot some of them down with his own rockets.

Convoys from the ground were trying to follow the C-2 around to engage them. But these were sitting ducks for the C-2s scanners, and then weapons to finish them off.

Derek flew over the airport to see how the other group was doing. It looked like their men were pinned down taking gunfire. He immediately made a pass at the enemy, and the C-2 crew scanned them senseless. The second pass dispatched the enemy force, and the friendly group pumped their fists into the air.

Kibble found himself wondering out loud. "Could it be that our guys don't know how to use scanners?"

Ed shook his head. "I'm seriously thinking they don't know."

Alexander peered into every horizon before speaking. "Don't stop now! Keep going until we've taken out the weapons over the entire city!"

Derek flipped it into high gear and began systematically covering every region of Castle City. It was a large area, but he knew it well, and within an hour, peace and tranquility reigned everywhere.

Alexander was on the radio with Sam, telling him to reorganize the army immediately, to regain control of the city.

Setting the radio down, he grinned, yet with an angry expression. "We're going to take this country back." He gripped and rattled his sword. "And then the world!"

Derek circled the city twice, finding no trouble spots. "That will do it." Alexander determined. "Take us to the airport, and then the capitol building."

At the airport Sam was dealing with crowds of patriots gathering to rejoin the military and be a part of this great rebellion. Several other generals came out of the woodwork and joined Sam in restructuring the branches of the military, after two years of occupation.

Ed passed out his remaining supply of scanners to the generals and promised to have more by the next day. When the time travelers drove up to the capitol building, most of their faithful staffers were waiting on the steps and cheered their arrival.

Alexander walked up to them and held up his arms. As silence reigned, he delivered a short message. "Thank you for coming!" The cheers took a minute to die down again. "Go home and tell everyone to come to work tomorrow morning!"

42

Everyone went home and had a blessed and serene night. The next day was going to be a new beginning for an oppressed group of people.

The time travelers met in Alexander's office that morning. All were there, including Lex and James, who hadn't known any of this was happening until that very morning when Alexander called. They sat beaming in their seats, after waking up to their old, high profile and happy lives.

Alexander remained standing while everyone else was seated, as was his custom to start meetings. "I welcome you all back to this table, after such a long and arduous plight to better the outcome of the world." He looked at James. "I know, James, that you missed a large part of our quest that led us through two great wars. I trust Lex has filled you in." James nodded, conveying a patented ministerial smile.

Alexander thumbed his sword handle, then lifted his chin. "Today we are going to discuss what is going on, and what is our next move." He pulled out his chair and took a seat.

No one initiated a conversation, so Alexander continued. "I am going to monitor closely the building up of our military and controlling more and more of this country. James, can you give us a feel of the situation in the rest of the country?"

"Indeed," James replied, "I've been following news coverage of our country. The middle eastern group of countries has taken over everywhere and ruled with an iron hand. I think now they still hold a grip in all areas except now this one."

Kibble jumped in. "So, what are the three countries in this alliance?"

James quickly answered. "Iran, Syria, and Lebanon. These three have joined hands with anti-freedom groups such as neo-Nazis. That's why the swastika in the flag."

Ed piped up with a question. "Do they have nuclear weapons?"

James pursed his lips as he glanced at Ed and everyone at the table. "They have control of our nuclear weapons."

Heads shook, and sighs were heard, but Lex would have none of it. "Wait a minute. It's not going to be that hard. We know where the nukes are, and we know our scanners will shut them down! We should actually knock them out first thing."

Alexander slapped the table. "This is going to be our next job! Not everyone has to go because it will be dangerous. But four should be there to cover scanner targets."

Kibble did not look excited, but he agreed. "Yes but remember we will end up having to scan hundreds of other weapons in the process of hitting the nukes."

Derek held up his hands. "Yes, we know the drill. Everything and everyone's going to come after us."

"Ok," Alexander weighed in. "This has got to be done now. I'm asking for volunteers."

No one budged, and all remained quiet. Finally, Derek raised a finger. "It goes without saying that I have to go. I'll just volunteer before I get the order."

Alexander snorted. "Well, I must stay to get this city to its feet. And really James has an important job here, and I don't think we should send Lex without him."

Kibble, Ed, and Chad bore somber looks, knowing that this may be the most dangerous mission they have ever been on.

"I have a suggestion." Kibble broke the silence. "Can we take about 10 F-4s along with us? That would even the odds a bit."

Alexander nodded. "That would be a very good idea, but I need to check the availability of F-4s. I'll do the best that I can."

43

Ed came shuffling into the airport lounge where Derek, Kibble, and Chad were waiting for him. "I have installed new scanners and anti-scanners in all ten of the F-4s. We're ready to go."

The 3 men reluctantly got up and started walking toward the C-2. This was the sign for all ten F-4 pilots to head to their solar powered jet fighters.

Derek, and every other pilot knew the three sites where nuclear weapons had been placed. Site A was 500 miles away, site B was 2,000 miles away, site C was 5,000 miles away.

As the C-2 crew loaded in, the F-4s took off on the runway. Derek lifted off quickly, going straight up to 4,000 feet. He then flew at top speed (500mph) to catch up with the F-4s. He eventually flew above the F-4 formation for safety.

Site A would be in northern Canada, were this the original time thread. Site B would be on the Oregon coast. Site C would be on the eastern Mexican seaboard.

Derek glanced at Kibble seated next to him. "We're going to start getting resistance soon."

Kibble confirmed. "We'll be ready. Just make sure you are ready at the scanner too."

Derek laughed. "Have you ever seen me not ready?"

Kibble returned a chuckle. "We can't get overconfident, you know."

Derek and the F-4s cruised at 450mph, and within minutes saw opposition coming. A group of 10 Russian-built fighters came up quickly on them. "2 o'clock!" Derek shouted. The enemy had already fired on them, but Derek and the other men scanned them furiously. Derek then fired a missile interceptor and noticed some of the F-4s doing the same thing. Apparently the F-4s had been scanning as well, because enemy fire stopped. The enemy planes were dead in the water and started disappearing in the wake of a combined missile attack. Within seconds the skies were clear.

Five minutes later their target came up. Derek lowered altitude along with the F-4s. He saw the target on the instrument panel and reached for the scanner. At the right time he pulled the trigger, along with the rest of the crew, and the F-4s. The scanners all registered that the nukes were incapacitated.

A cheer went up as everyone turned around and headed south toward site 2.

"That wasn't bad." Chad sounded optimistic.

"True," Ed responded, "but this was the least defended site. The others might be a lot more difficult to get to."

Kibble turned around. "As long as we keep scanning fast and accurate, those 2 sites will go down just as fast."

"Certainly, I hope you're right." Ed concurred. "The major advantage we have is their scanners can't touch us. Their missiles could get us if we aren't fast enough at scanning."

Three hours later, site 2 came up on the west coast. Immediately, two groups of 10 fighters apiece came up against them. The C-2 and F-4s fired scanners on first impulse, and then fired rockets and missiles. The Russian-made fighters were apparently scanning, but to no avail. By the time they were finished trying to scan the F-4s, they were already targeted by missiles and rockets.

"That's how it's done!" Derek shouted. "Timing is everything!"

The site 2 nukes were scanned by all, and then the group turned toward the southeast, and site 3. This site was 3,000 miles away, so the formation increased their speed to 500mph, in order to get there in 6 hours. This was a long trip, but not tedious. Opposition came after them nearly the whole way. One of the F-4s was hit but could still fly and keep up with the group.

On the approach to site 3, the enemy launched a massive attack, in overwhelming fashion. Everyone had to scan at the top of their ability to avoid annihilation. Two F-4s were hit, and the pilots had to eject. Derek saw this and took note of the parachutes' positions.

The group of F-4s and C-2 continued to scan at lightning speed, and finally caught up to the onslaught by the enemy. The combination of rocket and missile fire won the war of attrition. Every enemy jet fighter was destroyed, and the F-4s went in to scan site 3's nukes.

Derek took this chance to go after the downed pilots. He followed the coordinates to the very spots of parachute landings. Descending rapidly, he moved in on one parachute, landing softly.

Not far away was the pilot, who saw the C-2, and came running. The side door swung open, and the pilot climbed in with a smile on his face.

Derek then quickly buzzed straight up and toward the coordinates of the other parachute.

When he saw the yellow and green chute, he zoned in on it, but the pilot was not around.

"Look ahead!" Chad shouted. A group of enemy soldiers was marching along a road and had taken the pilot captive.

Derek jumped into reflex mode and went after the group. Coming up behind them, he nearly hit their heads with the bottom of the C-2. He looped around and went in again, this time strafing the ground behind them. They started running and abandoned the captive pilot.

As Derek landed, the pilot jumped up and down, pumping his fist in the air. Crawling into the C-2, he thanked Derek over and over for rescuing him.

For Derek, the whole thing was worth it just to see the happy faces of the two rescued pilots.

He quickly caught up to the F-4s and began the long trip home.

44

The flight home was uneventful. Apparently the Arabs realized their disadvantage, and didn't want to lose any more planes and men.

Alexander was in contact with Sam, who had good news about large numbers of recruits into the military. They already had groups of soldiers patrolling the city, and the enemy was out of sight, if not out of town.

By the time the group reached Castle City, they had been gone for 24 hours, and were exhausted. Everyone shook hands and congratulated one another for a successful sortie. They then trudged home and flopped into bed.

Ed had managed to get quite a number of volunteers to help him make one thousand scanners in one day. They were then dispersed to Army and Airforce personnel. He would continue making more scanners for several more days.

Everything that had a scanner also had an anti-scanner in it. This would give them the upper hand in any military encounter.

Alexander put Chad to work as the Mayor of Castle City, since the position was vacant. He understood, however, that he was a time travel member, and that took precedence over his regular job. He was good with that. Time travel was beginning to get into his blood.

James and Lex kept busy with church business, but they also were time travel group members, and were to drop and run if needed for a mission.

Derek was involved with virtually everything in time travel, mostly because he was the pilot of the C-2. But also because he was the genius who discovered time travel, and he was constantly making improvements in the technical aspects of it. He also did daily checks of the future just to keep aware of any surprises coming up.

Alexander desperately wanted to get and keep control of the country, as this would maintain peace and prosperity all over the world. There were always power-hungry groups with agendas to take over the most powerful and influential country in the world. He knew they had to keep on their toes to ward off any plots to bring them down.

He sat in his office staring at a map of the middle east, and the 3 countries who formed an alliance against them. He noticed that all 3 were either bordering each other or very close.

Then came a knock at his door, followed by the door opening, and in walked Reverend James Jacobs. Alexander stood to greet him. "I had forgotten that I gave you a call. You are just the man I want to see." He motioned for James to sit at the table with him.

He started right in on his concern. "These three countries who formed an alliance against us… I've been studying them on the map, and they're in very close proximity to one another. What do they have in common, and why would they want to take over our country?"

James, who held a history minor in his native time thread, nonetheless, had done a lot of studying, and knew a lot about different cultures. He scratched his head and held his chin in thought.

"These are radical Muslim states, who hate anything to do with the Jewish or Christian faiths."

He focused on Alexander for a moment. "They are willing to do anything to bring us down as a country, because we are a symbol of what they hate. They also want the opportunity to grab power by taking over the government."

Alexander nodded but had a puzzled look on his face. "What is the connection between them and what they call neo-Nazis?"

James smiled and folded his hands. "This is an unlikely alliance to be sure. Actually, the connection is money, but they both hate the same things. The neo-Nazis and other hate groups in many parts of the world have connections to sales of weapons.

That is something these 3 countries all seek, so they formed a union to fight for similar goals. Their attack on us is a direct result of their goals."

Alexander rubbed the back of his neck and smiled in frustration. "I have an idea how to get them out of our country, but it's going to require time travel and dangerous work."

He stood and shook James' hand. "Tell Lex we will be meeting at 3pm today to discuss this."

James smiled and nodded. "Will see you then."

45

The time travel meeting convened at 3pm, with all members present. Alexander actually sat down with the others to start the meeting. "Folks," he seemed calm and collected, "we are here to discuss a quicker solution to this crisis. Engaging in warfare like we are now doing, will be a prolonged and protracted campaign." He looked around the table. "I think a time-travel solution would be much faster and better."

Chad spoke up. "Are you proposing going back to the beginning of the invasion, to stop it from happening?"

Alexander nodded. "Essentially, yes I am. It would be much easier to stop it then than to battle it now."

Lex jumped in. "Hear me out. If we go back and fix this before it happens, that puts our counterparts in a good position." She looked into every set of eyes. "Where does that put us ourselves? I'll tell you where. Not here. Somewhere out there in time, looking for a home. I want to stay in my home, not fix things up for my counterpart."

Alexander looked around. "Does anyone have an answer?"

"I do." Derek spoke in a calm, quiet voice. "That's been our problem all along. We would go back and fix something, and then when we check into the future again, our counterparts are there living a good life, so we have to find somewhere else to go."

He took a deep breath and smiled. "Ok, I have the solution." Eyebrows raised around the table. The silence was deafening. "I call it the 'Time Jump'. When we go to the future to see if we fixed it… as soon as we get there, we jump back to where we just came from, and then jump back to the future immediately. That does something to us that fits us right into our future." He glanced at everyone. "No counterparts. It's really us."

Alexander and Kibble exchanged glances. Ed had a sly grin while shaking his head. "Derek this sounds like some kind of fairy tale. Where did you get this?"

Derek folded his hands and rested them on the table. "From experimentation. I know this because I've tested it a bunch of times."

Kibble smiled. "I've known you long enough to trust anything you say. If you believe it, and it looks like you do, then I trust that it's true."

Everyone around the table agreed and placed their trust in Derek.

Alexander laughed and gave the thumbs up sign. "If this is true, it's going to be fantastic. Let's try it…tomorrow morning at 8am."

Ed interjected. "This is all well and good, but exactly what are we going to do to fix this?"

Alexander leaned forward. "We are going to go around and scan all of their weapons. That will put them out of business. No invasion".

Heads nodded in agreement. "Sounds too easy." Ed grinned in disbelief.

46

All time travelers were present standing next to the C-2 at the airport. Alexander handed Derek a piece of paper with the date of the invasion roughly two years ago.

The group stood around him while he deliberated last minute instructions.

"Let's remember this is going to be the beginning of the invasion. They will just be getting started and will be vulnerable to attack. That's going to be us. Keep the scanners in your hands and shoot anything that looks like or could be a weapon. We can do this without anyone even seeing us. Don't be obvious unless you have to. Got it? Let's go!"

With everyone loaded, Derek started the engine and flew straight up. At 2,000 feet he hovered while he programmed the trip. "Ok, here we go." He announced.

Within seconds the scene changed as everyone peered out the windows.

"We're going down for a better view." He announced, and then dropped smoothly out of the sky. Ed scrutinized the scene below. "If you remember, we were trying to fight off the Chinese. Guess what…those are Chinese down there."

"So how did the Arabs get here?" Chad sounded puzzled.

"My guess is this." Kibble expounded. "The Chinese broke through into the country, and then left. At that point the Arabs filled the vacuum."

Derek followed the line of reasoning and programed for a week into the future. Suddenly the Chinese were gone, but no one was there. He tried one more week in the future, and there they were…the Arabs and the odd-looking flag with the swastika on it.

"What do you know?" Kibble declared. "They have arrived."

"This is it!" Alexander blurted out. "Start scanning everything in sight!"

The crew targeted vehicles, guns, and equipment, and Derek moved on to new areas. They moved through the city doing this for several hours. Finally, the Arabs caught on and tried to attack them from the ground, but they were scanned before they could get a shot off. Planes and jets came from the sky but were targeted way before they got near. When they came upon heavy weaponry, Derek fired cannons, rockets, or missiles at it.

As they encompassed the entire city with scanners, the Arabs got angrier and more desperate, and threw everything at them, to no avail. The time travelers could see them on the ground yelling and shaking fists at them.

"Pay no attention to them!" Alexander shouted to Derek. "We will just continue scanning until they are gone!"

Derek did exactly that. He flew everywhere, and everyone in the C-2 scanned anything suspicious looking.

Being scan-proof turned out to be a cakewalk for the attackers. Everything they encountered was scanned into submission, and soon the entire city was taken back.

"Ok," Alexander jumped in, head over to the capitol building and see what's going on there."

In 5 minutes, when they flew overhead, he lamented. "Everyone went home when the invasion began."

Kibble piped up. "Probably better for us to head back and see how this affected the future."

"And I'd like to see how Derek's Time jump trick works." Ed chuckled.

Alexander nodded. "Sounds like the best course of action."

Derek flew high and hovered while programming a trip for two years ahead." He looked over his shoulder to address the crew. "We'll go forward, and then quickly back here again, then just as quickly back there again."

Everyone nodded and agreed, so Derek turned and started the process. Almost instantly they popped into the future. Without hesitation, he thrust. back into the past. Then he deliberately rushed forward to their current time.

Stopping and staring, everyone was silent for a moment.

"Very good." Alexander calmly began to issue his next order. "Let's go see what we've got here."

47

Derek landed the C-2 like so many times before on the lawn in front of the building. Alexander reached for the door. "Kibble and Ed let's go". The three men walked up the sidewalk and steps to the door, and casually stepped inside.

Inside the first floor did not look the same as usual. Different personnel filled the room, and none seemed friendly. At the 5th floor the elevator door opened, and the men stepped out. To their surprise, there were no guards at the door. They just strolled across the room to the head office, and Alexander opened the door.

Scanners in hand, they rushed around the corner and walked into a room full of soldiers with rifles on their backs. The 3 began scanning in earnest, as the armed men unshouldered their rifles and pulled their triggers. When nothing happened, they reached for their swords and rushed toward Alexander, Kibble, and Ed, who all had pistols, but Alexander preferred his sword. So, six men with swords attacked one with a sword… Alexander the Great. Of the three directly in front of him, he kicked the one on the left while thrusting through the one in the middle. Ducking, he avoided the man on the right trying to decapitate him, then dispatched him with a sword to the gut. Two men behind them jabbed at Alexander with their swords, but he stabbed the right one while grabbing the left one's arm. With his leg, he pushed the man clear across the room where his head slammed against a desk corner. He then leaned backward, avoiding the jab of the 6th man, and thrusting him through the chest.

Kibble and Ed had just drawn their pistols and were looking for targets.

They suddenly realized the men they had fought were Chinese. "Let's get out of here while we can!" Alexander shouted as he sprinted toward the stairwell. They ran down the stairs, all the way to the first floor, carrying scanners out into the open. There several men tried to shoot them but got scanned first. Alexander broke into a full run out the front door with Kibble and Ed lagging behind a bit. The group in the C-2 saw them, and Derek started the engine, lifting off just as the three escapees jumped in.

As Derek flew straight up, the other time travelers scanned through the windows for all they were worth. He didn't stop elevating till 5,000 feet, and then programmed a trip two years back, when they had just finished off the Arabs.

"Anyone want to explain what just happened?" Alexander threw out the question.

Kibble volunteered as he turned in his seat. "The Chinese saw how we kicked out the Arabs, and they came right back to keep us from grabbing power."

Ed nodded. "That's about the size of it. Now we have to invent a scheme to get rid of them."

All was quiet for a moment while everyone thought but couldn't come up with an idea. Then Chad spoke up. "OK, when you guys first got here there was a good king in power. What did you say his name was?"

Alexander's eyebrows raised. "Why didn't I think of that? Go ahead and finish your thought."

Chad went on. "Well, I just thought that if you went back to this time of prosperity, maybe you could get a foot in the door to control rebellion like we're experiencing now."

Lex quickly spoke her piece. "It does seem like we are just sliding out of control here no matter what we do."

James picked up the thought. "With this advanced scanner technology, we should be able to rapidly gain the upper hand anywhere in the world."

Kibble frowned and shook his head. "We are going to run into our counterparts. Dennis Carrigan showed Alexander the ropes, and then we all made the transition into our positions."

Derek suddenly snapped his fingers loudly. "That's it!" He excitedly scanned around the group. "The Time Jump." He became tongue tied for a moment. "It should work like a charm!"

He grabbed at his seat and flipped himself around. "Listen up! We'll do the Time Jump just ahead of when we first arrived here while Dennis Carrigan was still in power."

Kibble squeezed in. "We'll be reliving our great moment of celebration and destiny, when people knew who we were before we knew them!"

Alexander smiled. "I'd be willing to go through that again just to have another chance at spreading peace, prosperity, and happiness."

Everyone voiced their approval and shook hands all around. They had another chance for success!

48

The sequence had been programed, and Derek waited for the nod, while still hovering at 5,000 feet.

Alexander spoke before the trip started. "Remember we are arriving for the first time, as far as they are concerned. Try to act genuine like we all did the real first time. Don't tell anyone about this being our second time around. They really wouldn't understand anyway. So, I think we are ready to go. No need to carry your scanners. This is a peaceful society. Let's go!"

Derek hit the key, and propelled the C-2 to 2028, then quickly forward to 2030, and then back again to 2028. They still hovered at 5,000 feet, so he began the descent to the capitol building. On the way down everyone took note of the loved flag of the United American Republics.

The C-2 gently landed on the grass. This aircraft was one noticeable difference between the first arrival and the second. The first time they were travelling in the helicopter. The other noticeable difference was The presence of Chad and Ed this time. They all got out and started walking toward the building. This time no one really noticed them because of the absence of the helicopter.

Everyone followed Alexander through the door, and immediately they noticed all the people they worked with and knew well, but of course they didn't know them yet.

Alexander went straight to the elevator, and all seven people stepped into it. On the top floor, the doors open, and all were surprised that no guards were there.

The last part of the trip was across the floor to Dennis Carrigan's office. Alexander walked straight to the door and turned around. I will go into his office alone, but the rest of you can wait here inside the door. Come in when I call you. Hopefully he's in there.

He turned and walked straight into the office. Busy at his desk, was Dennis Carrigan, who didn't even see he had a visitor. Alexander then lightly knocked on the wall. Raising his eyes, Dennis looked at Alexander and smiled. "Hello, sir. Can I help you?"

Alexander returned the smile. "In fact, yes you can. Have you heard of a story about five time-travelers who founded this country long ago? Dennis' interest was aroused, and he stared at Alexander, as he answered. "Yes, I know all about that story. What do you know of it?"

Smiling again, Alexander replied. "More than you realize." He reached down and pulled his sword part way out, and back in again.

"We've come to visit for a while."

Dennis didn't move but stared at the man in front of him. He then forced himself to speak. "Who, then, are you, sir?"

"They call me Alexander." I was born in 323BC. But I'm here now for as long as you need me. And my friends." He signaled for the others to come out.

As the time travelers stood in front of him, Dennis stood, grinning. "Would you all come have a seat at my table?"

49

Dennis sat at the table, and the time travelers sat around and across from him. He started the conversation with a laugh and said. "Just let me guess who you are. Lex the redhead for sure, but then you are the only woman…not fair. And you must be Professor Kibble." Kibble nodded, "And you are Derek, the genius young man. I believe you are Reverend James Jacobs. As for the other two, I am unfamiliar."

Kibble offered an introduction. "This is Ed Worth, a brilliant scientist, and this is Chad Power, who was a city mayor when we found him along the way."

"I always hoped to see you folks". Dennis spoke from the heart. "But I truly didn't really believe it would happen."

He went on. "So, what is it that brings you this far into the future?"

Alexander lowered his head for a second and replied. "We've been searching for a home in time travel, and just haven't found one yet."

Dennis held up a hand. "Let me stop you right there. Look no further, because you've just found your home. Did you know you are all historical icons? You are famous! You are in all the history books written up as the founders of this country!"

Alexander appeared tongue tied for a moment. Dennis continued. "It's only fitting that you should stay here to enjoy the fruits of your labor."

Alexander nodded pleasantly. "We all surely appreciate this kindness."

Dennis smiled and gestured to everyone at the table. "I have an offer for all of you sitting here that I hope you won't refuse. First of all, I will be retiring very soon, and have no heir to pass my kingship down to. Why don't you, Alexander, take my place? You can then run the same country that you founded. As for the rest of you, we will have quality positions for all of you."

Alexander beamed with satisfaction. "Dennis, we will all accept this gracious offer before you change your mind."

He chuckled. "But I will need Kibble as my right-hand man."

Dennis nodded. "The choices are yours to make! But the only thing I would like in return is to do some time traveling."

Everyone got a laugh out of that. "We can definitely accommodate you with that." Kibble chortled.

Dennis raised a hand to the group. "Welcome to the United American Republics!"

Everyone applauded and thanked this generous king.

Alexander shook his hand. "Right now, all we need are places to stay and a place to park our aircraft."

Dennis nodded. "I'll see to that right now. And we'll schedule a day for me to show you how I run this place. I know you're already an experienced emperor."

Alexander spoke of his gratefulness. "It's hard to express how beholden we are to you. We feel like we have finally come home!"

50

The time travelers were given separate lavish quarters. James and Lex shared a nice place, and the remainder of them shared a spacious home. The C-2 was taken to a nearby airfield and placed in a hangar.

Each one of them was given a state-of-the-art cell phone for communication convenience.

The next morning Alexander, Kibble, Ed, Chad, and Derek were up to the kitchen table sipping coffee. Alexander shook his head in disbelief. "It's tough to think this is the same time thread as we just came from, which was invaded and overrun."

Kibble returned a head shake. "Yes. We'll have to run a tight ship in order to maintain a fair and orderly world."

"Absolutely." Alexander acknowledged. "And Ed, you can spend most of your time upgrading and expanding the weapons shutdown system."

Ed agreed. "If I had the time and the resources, I could really put a wrench into every attempted rebellion."

Alexander smiled and took a sip. "That's exactly what we need. Speaking of need." He elaborated. "Chad, we need to find a good spot for you. Do you want to govern a republic, or work closely with my office?"

Chad sat his cup down. "If I want to stay with the time traveler group, I should work with your office. I think I'd much prefer that."

"Agreed." Alexander held up his mug.

"And Derek, are we looking at keeping you in time travel testing and research, like we have been doing?"

Derek grinned and nodded. "That's punching my ticket."

Alexander then looked to professor Kibble. "How about you? Do you still like spending most of your time in the lab, or in government?"

Kibble laughed as he sipped. "I'll put in my time with government, but I'm a scientist at heart. I still need the lab."

Alexander's phone buzzed, and he examined it. "Wow. Looks like I'm going in for my one day of training." He snickered into his drink. "Don't worry. I'll try to act as inexperienced as possible, so I don't give away any knowledge that I've been doing this for two years already."

Everyone laughed.

At the office, Dennis was amazed at how quickly Alexander caught on to everything. It was hard for Alexander to start a new relationship with someone he already knew well, but he accomplished the job.

Dennis scheduled Alexander for a press conference and an interview so the public could get properly informed about what was taking place. This was not Alexander's favorite pastime, but he still had fun with it.

Dennis was very anxious to retire, and actually encouraged speeding up the process of Alexander taking over. He somehow had complete faith in Alexander's ability, morality, and judgement.

Alexander finally got the time to drop by to see James and Lex one morning. They sat on couches for a little discussion.

"I came over to just find out what you're thinking." He directed the question to James. "Do you want to stay with the same church, or go into some other field?"

James laughed before answering. "I've always been a preacher, and I don't want to change now."

"Great." Alexander replied. "We'll check to see if the same church is available for you. Or would you prefer to do your own business?"

James chuckled again. "I wouldn't mind a little help. It never hurts to have a king on your side."

Alexander directed his attention to Lex. "So, Lex, how do you want your life to go?"

Lex crossed her legs and flipped her hair back. "Oh, I'll stick with the time travelers. You guys need someone to keep you in line. As far as another job goes, I can just help James with church stuff."

Alexander didn't try to hold back laughter. "Sounds really good. We do value your input with anything."

51

The time travelers got the opportunity to start over again and didn't waste it. No one let on to the fact that this was their second go at it, and they were able to avoid a number of pitfalls in the process.

This period of peace and prosperity was good for all. However, Alexander made sure there was significant headway made with the shutdown system. Ed pushed himself to explore every possible avenue for advancement and came up with several gems. Alexander started developing great respect for Ed and his abilities.

Kibble also made great progress on several projects, mostly with time travel. He worked with Derek, and together they did some amazing things.

James got his old church back and had a tremendous advantage knowing the outcomes of problems ahead of time. He was in his element as a preacher and pastor, and also had the support of a good wife.

Lex relished the time she could live surrounded by modern comforts, after spending so much of the last two years in constant privation and danger. But there was a part of her which thrived on challenges faced with the time travel group.

Chad developed into a communications link between Alexander and the other branches of government. He enjoyed and learned a lot acting the role of a liaison.

After six months in office, Alexander felt he was making real progress establishing control of world governments for the purpose of advancing human rights. He learned how to be firm when he had to and be 'nice' when he could afford to.

After a long absence, the time travelers held a meeting to keep abreast with current events and issues. Alexander welcomed everyone to his office and stood for a brief time while the others were seated.

"Things have been going smoothly for a long while, but now it has come to my attention that there is an issue in our original time thread. Derek does daily checks in several time threads, and only yesterday found something that we are very concerned about. Derek."

He sat at the head of the table while Derek started a report. "Yesterday I discovered that in our native time thread, they are on the verge of world war…probably nuclear, which would mean total world annihilation." He scooted his chair out a bit and loosened an uncomfortable tie. "I ran some percentages which showed that there is a 75% chance of world nuclear war, unless we can find a way to change that."

Kibble folded his hands and hunched over a little. "Can you give us any information about what this is all about?"

Derek spoke about what he found. "The whole world is aligned in a faceoff about China's control of international waters in the South China Sea. Neither side is budging, and fighting has already taken place. This will soon lead to a nuclear interchange."

Ed shared his thoughts. "It would certainly be better to stop this before it goes to nuclear war than to wait for world destruction and then go back for another try."

"I have a crazy thought that just might work." Chad jumped in. "With these high-tech scanners we may be able to talk Washington DC into making a bold move to show who's boss. That would make the Chinese rethink their course of action."

Alexander held out an empty hand. "What's the bold move?"

"The US and its allies gets together the largest military fleet in history and sails straight into the south China sea. They sail past Hong Kong, past Taiwan, and up to Shanghai. The Chinese are forced to attack, and when they do, the scanners send them down to defeat. They are obliged to cooperate, and the crisis is solved."

"Wow!" Kibble squeezed his lower jaw and shook his head. "When you said bold, you meant it!"

Everyone seemed stumped, and silence prevailed. Suddenly the voice of reason spoke. Lex took the floor. "You guys can't be afraid to do the right thing here. What are we faced with? Nuclear holocaust! We also know that our scanners can stop anything, and I think the odds are much better with Chad's idea!"

"When I think about this," Ed began, "that sounds like a perfect plan. It's destined to succeed, and the Chinese can do nothing else but cooperate."

Alexander entered the conversation. "Unless someone has a better idea, or a reason this wouldn't work, I think this is what we should do."

Everyone looked at each other and shook their heads.

52

Ed had made several scanner improvements, one of which was auto-scan. This was effective in automatically scanning in a 360-degree spherical circle. Friendly weapons didn't get scanned because they each had a chip which matched a certain code. This, however, was not 100% foolproof. The hand-held scanners still had to be used.

The time travelers stood outside the aircraft, and Alexander stood to speak for a moment.

"We are headed for the White House lawn again. It seems the best spot to be recognized right away. Auto-scan, of course, will be used, but we need to pretend we don't have it. Our objective is to speak with the President, but if that fails, we will try to find General Scott. He was a big help last time, and I hope he's still around. Are there any questions?"

Chad spoke up. "What if no one cooperates? What is the plan then?"

"I hate to think of that happening, but we'll find some way to scan them into submission. Ok let's go!"

The C-2 passengers loaded and buckled, after which Derek hit the sky about a thousand feet up. "Ready with the scanners!" He warned, and then flipped the switch.

The scene changed abruptly, as they now hovered above the white house to attract attention. It worked. Within seconds there were security and military shooting at them from the ground. No weapons seemed to be firing, however, with auto-scanner and seven other scanners going.

Derek smoothly descended and landed nicely on the lawn. "Let's go!" Alexander gave the word, and

everyone bailed and walked together as a group toward the building.

A gathering crowd of opposition poured through gates and doors, pointing their guns. Someone called out. "Stop! Go no further or we'll shoot!" The time travelers paid no heed but kept trudging forward. "Ok I warned you!" Came the call. They all raised their guns to fire, but the time travelers had already fired their scanners, and the guns facing them were like toys. The men looked at their weapons and tried to unjam them, but nothing worked.

Finally, Alexander and company stopped and stood in a row a few feet away from the gunmen. One man with a gun threw it on the ground and ran toward the seven time-travelers. He pulled a knife from his belt and raised his arm as he ran. Alexander drew his sword, and without moving his feet, whipped it in a sideways motion, flipping the knife cleanly out of the man's hand. He then stuck out a foot and tripped the man, who fell flat on his face.

Alexander then held up one hand and spoke. "May I say something?"

Silence prevailed, as he continued. "We are here as friends. We wish to speak to the president."

A spokesman for the other group answered. "The president isn't here right now. Who are you, and what do you want?"

Alexander slipped his sword back home and gave a response. "We are the same group who helped you two years ago to avoid nuclear war. You are in danger once again."

Laughter came from the crowd. "Those crackpots who said they were time travelers?"

"Take us to General Scott." Alexander was beginning to lose patience.

Someone whispered into the spokesman's ear. He suddenly stood back and pushed the man away. He then marched straight toward Alexander. "You are under arrest for trespassing!" He tried to grab Alexander's hands to cuff him, but Alexander simply slipped his hand out and punched the man in the nose. He fell helplessly to the ground.

"Once more I ask. Take us to General Scott!"

The man who did the whispering stepped forward. "If you will follow me, I'll take you to him."

Alexander nodded and started following the man, and the rest kept pace.

53

Alexander spoke softly to Derek, who ran back and jumped into the C-2. He took off immediately, flying straight up to avoid having the aircraft confiscated. The others ducked into a vehicle which started up and drove away.

Derek was 1,000 feet up following the car all the way. The car parked next to a two-story building, and the passengers disembarked. Derek hovered.

The man who drove led the way into the building, and up the stairs, showing Alexander the office of General Scott. Alexander thanked him and knocked on the door.

Soon the door opened, and there stood a wide-eyed General Scott. "I don't believe it. I never thought I'd see you people again." He opened the door wide. "Come in, please."

The group filed in and stood next to his desk, as the general closed the door. "I know we are dangerously close to nuclear war, and I assume that's why you're here."

Alexander nodded. "We tried the white house again, but they said the president wasn't there. Is he the same man as last time we were here?"

"I'm afraid not." The general sat down and folded his hands. "This president may not cooperate with you. We may have to go rogue again."

Alexander leaned over the desk. "Would it be worth it to call him and give it a try?"

General Scott grinned and frowned at the same time. He picked up his phone and dialed a number. "Mr. President, it's General Scott. I've got the time travelers here to help us win this thing. I implore you to talk with them. Would you see them?"

The group could hear angry speech coming through the receiver and began shaking their heads. Then the general looked at the phone and back to Alexander. "He hung up on me. That's your answer, gentlemen."

Alexander grabbed a chair and sat down next to the desk. The group followed suit. Kibble scooted forward. "We're going to have to do this on our own just like last time. Are you in on this with us?"

"Absolutely." Came the reply. "In fact, my home is still open as a base for you if needed."

"Yes, that would be best." Alexander went on. "In fact, we have an aircraft hovering overhead as we speak."

"Oh!" the general grabbed a sticky pad and jotted down his address. "Just in case you don't remember. I'll be there in a few hours. The apartment above the garage is still open. I'll see you there."

Alexander stood. "Before we leave, I'm curious why you didn't keep using the scanners we gave you."

General Scott smiled. "Our famous congress and president voted against using scanners because it was an invasion of rights. I'm surprised they didn't vote out weapons altogether. We could fight our enemies with speeches!"

As he turned to leave, Alexander spoke parting words. "If this weren't so serious, that would be funny."

The time travelers exited General Scott's office and navigated downstairs and out to the street. Derek saw them and zoomed down to the street, landing directly in the center of the street until everyone was loaded. Traffic patiently waited, not knowing what the C-2 was.

Alexander handed Derek the address, and in a few seconds they shoved off. It took only a couple minutes to get to General Scott's back yard where they enjoyed a soft landing on the lawn.

Everyone enjoyed strolling around the yard for a moment, before heading up to the apartment.

Lounging on couches was good relaxation. Someone made coffee for all, and the group was ready for a discussion.

54

Alexander sat at the center of a couch sipping coffee. "Well, we need to discuss a plan of action. Any ideas off the top?"

"It strikes me oddly," Kibble offered, "that we have to keep bailing these guys out, when they won't even use the scanners that we leave for them!"

"Exactly." Ed added. "I mean, are they trying to lose a nuclear war?"

Chad agreed. "They could have taken control of the world long ago, but no, it's a human rights violation to scan a weapon?"

"Don't look at it that way". Lex could take only so much. "Sure, there are a lot of idiots in government! But think of the hundreds of millions of innocent people who have to live with the laws made by the fruitcakes! This is where we came from, and are we going to fight for the people? No one else is fighting for them, so we have to!"

"I'll have to agree." James jumped in. "Not just because she's my wife." Chuckles came from all around.

"Maybe someone will start getting the picture after they see us taking control of the situation. Maybe they will start electing people that will fight for them."

"To put in my two cents," Derek spoke up, "yes, we have to try to make this right. They are taking over a shipping channel in international waters. That's like allowing piracy to go on and on."

Alexander raised his hand. "Ok, do we have a consensus? Or does someone still disagree?"

Kibble made a clarification. "Yes, my anger is directed at the leadership. So, with that in mind, I agree we need to take action." Ed and Chad nodded in conformity.

"Alright, do we need to focus on taking out their nukes, or conventional weapons?" Alexander posed this question. "Definitely nukes to start with." Kibble sounded confident. "Then of course we go to their conventional weapons to demoralize them."

"My understanding," Ed added, "is that General Scott can provide us with nuclear installation sites."

Derek added to this. "From my research, most of their sites are located near or in Taiwan, and the interior of China. That's where we need specifics from General Scott."

"I can add this much as well." Alexander expounded. "We are going to want to get started with this no later than tomorrow morning. The longer we wait, the more danger we are all in."

Lex weighed in with a thought. "Some of us really don't want to go on a dangerous mission like this. But I have to say that all of our scanners are needed, and we need to suck it up and do our jobs."

"I'd like to add this." Ed began. "If we are scanning properly, and we have auto-scan going, we should be safe anywhere we go."

Ed spoke again. "One more thing. If General Scott has a government computer in his home, I could stay here to hook up the shutdown system to satellite."

"Sounds like it's a go!" Alexander concluded. "We'll just wait for him to get here before finalizing things, and tomorrow we'll execute our plan."

55

The time travelers performed some R & R for a couple of hours before General Scott knocked at the door.

"Is this a good time?" Kibble smiled and nodded. "Yes it is!" He swung open the door.

The general walked in and pulled up a chair close to the coffee table. He spoke while sitting. "Just to let you know, the president told me that if you use scanners on the Chinese, you will be committing a crime." He looked at Alexander. "And if I help you in any way, it's over for me too. So let me start out by asking you folks. If I assist you, will you take me back with you to your home?"

Alexander didn't even hesitate. That will pose no problem. Count yourself in."

General Scott loosened his tie and breathed a sigh of relief. He looked at Ed. "I am assuming that you'll need to adjust things with our computers." Ed nodded. The general continued. "There's one in my house. You can come over any time."

Alexander sat on the edge of the couch. "We need to get this done tomorrow morning. Does that work for you?"

"Certainly, but I wonder if I might go along with you? You may have to make an abrupt exit, and I don't want to miss out. My career and my life here are over."

Alexander smiled. "Do not worry. You'll be safe. We'll definitely take you with us." Alexander paused. "Is there anyone you need to bring along? You married?"

The general shook his head. "My wife passed away, and the kids are off doing their own thing. Oh, by the way, just call me Ben from now on."

Alexander folded his hands as if in thought. "Very good." He then gripped his sword as he continued. "Let me brief you on our mission tomorrow. We will all ride in the C-2 and transport ourselves to China. Can you give us specifics on their nuke locations?"

Ben nodded affirmatively. "Yes, I do have them."

Alexander clapped his hands. "Ed and Derek need to know them. As for the rest of us, all we will do is scan the heck out of everything in sight, and not in sight."

He saw a look of concern on Ben's face. "Don't worry, we have what is called 'auto-scan'. This gets 99 percent of their weapons. So, we only need to catch the remaining one percent. If we all scan hard, that's going to be a done deal."

Ben's eyes widened. "That's an amazing weapon. I see why you have so much confidence."

"So, when we finish," Kibble stepped in, "we'll need to take our leave…scram out of there."

Ben added a thought. "The president is going to have to decide on his own what to do. I'd say if he doesn't step up and do the right thing, he ought to be impeached. I'll tell you, most of the people will be with us on this."

Lex suddenly delivered a message. "It goes without saying that the Russians, Iranians, North Koreans, etcetera, might have to be dealt with. But I really think after they see what happens to China, they won't do anything."

Ben vigorously nodded. "I concur with that. I think you are doing the right thing here. The rest of the world will follow China." Chad chipped in. "So, if we do our part, and the US president does nothing, it will be all for naught? Am I missing something here?"

Kibble provided the reply. "Remember that we keep track of what's happening here daily. If we're required to come back, so be it."

Ben appeared confident. "I have no doubt that we'll get it done tomorrow. So, Ed, do you want to work with my government computer?"

"Sure thing." Ed replied.

Ben stood and eyed Alexander. "I'll print off two copies of the nuclear weapons sites, and send them with Ed."

Alexander stood and shook hands with Ben. "Let us know when you're up and around tomorrow."

Ben and Ed left, and the group sat looking at each other.

"I suppose we can retire early so we're on our game tomorrow." James made a suggestion, which everyone followed.

56

Things started moving around 7am. Everyone got up and had breakfast. Ben came over prepared for the day. He seemed impressed with the whole operation...the team comradery, the C-2, the high-tech scanners, and the plan of attack. To him this was Armageddon, the day of reckoning. To the time travelers, it seemed like just another day at the office. It was difficult for him to grasp, but he went along feeling secure.

Everyone boarded the aircraft in the back yard, while Derek double checked the transport data. Scanners were passed out, and Ben was briefed to their operation.

Alexander stood for a word before departure. "Derek is taking us to several sites in the interior of the country, followed by several sites in and around Taiwan. Do not be concerned about where exactly we are. Just do your scanning, taking it seriously, and we will be alright. Good luck to all of us with this all-important mission."

Alexander sat down, and Derek commenced with rapid transport to China. "Here we go!" He warned, just before flipping the switch. Instantly they were there. Chinese nuclear weapons sat just below them. "Start scanning!" Ed yelled, and everyone jumped out of their seats, rushing to a window and began scanning in earnest. Ben joined the crowd, doing his part.

"Auto scan on?" Ed queried. "Affirmative!" Derek returned.

The rocket launchers were not in plain sight, of course, but everyone knew they were underground, and scanned every square inch of the area below. Derek moved around in a fast, methodical way to make it easy to scan. Soon the area was finished, and he quickly went on to the next programmed address.

Instantly they were transported to a different address, and began scanning. Everyone did the same thing, Derek moved in the same pattern, and the scanners developed a pattern of action.

This continued for several more interior sites, but Derek and the crew performed exactly the same at every site. Before long, Derek made an announcement. "Now moving to Taiwan!"

Instantly the scene changed, but they knew they were just above a nuclear launcher that was buried underground. The group scanned like there was no tomorrow, which was true should they fail. Every objective they achieved by sharing info and responsibility.

Site by site, they did the same thing. Suddenly something was different. Derek notified them. "Incoming missiles! Scanning!" When incoming missiles were scanned, something definitely happened. They exploded. That happened about six times at the same site. They saw all the aircraft, but they turned and beelined in the opposite direction.

The C-2 was not seriously challenged as it continued its routine combing of the nuclear launching sites. Several sites were completed in Taiwan and the coast to China. Suddenly Derek announced. "This is the last one!" That seemed to inspire everyone to work even harder and faster than usual.

But aircraft approached, and from a distance, fired on the C-2. With the spherical auto-scanner, the missiles were toast anyway, and they all exploded nearly at the same time. Derek fired some missiles of his own at the retreating aircraft. Within a few seconds, two jet fighters were blown to pieces.

Derek did not say this ahead of time, but he transported them directly to an air force base. "Start scanning!" Ed yelled. "Shoot all aircraft and weapons."

This went very fast, as their targets were visible on the ground. The aircraft and weapons would be permanently disabled until being reverse scanned to normal operation.

They were transported to a total of three airfields, and shut down hundreds, even thousands of planes. Then the announcement came. "We are returning to our own time thread now." A cheer swelled in the C-2.

57

Instantly the C-2 was transported back to Castle City and the Capitol building. Another cheer rang out in the C-2. as Derek descended to the ground.

This was all new to Ben, who was not even familiar with this country or what time period it was.

On the ground, Alexander gave a short speech. "Job well done by a group of experts. Take some time off for vacationing, or whatever suits you best. Derek, keep checking back with the time thread we just left. This may not be over. Ben, if you want to come with me, we can discuss some options for you.

Everyone went their own way to forget about scanners and nuclear threats until the next time duty calls. General Ben Scott starts a new life in a much freer country, with a leader who looks out after the people, and not his own advancement.

The United American Republics has never been a better place to live. Alexander and Ben Scott sit in the King's office and look out the window over a free and fair land.

Ben smiles and shakes his head. "You know, I just feel it in my bones. Everything here is ten times better than the place I just left. I think I'll stay here."

Alexander leans back in his chair and puts his feet on the desk. "Good choice." He answers with a grin.

HISTORY OF THE AUTHOR

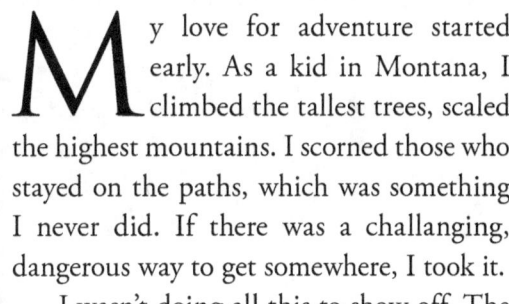

My love for adventure started early. As a kid in Montana, I climbed the tallest trees, scaled the highest mountains. I scorned those who stayed on the paths, which was something I never did. If there was a challanging, dangerous way to get somewhere, I took it.

I wasn't doing all this to show off. The act of jumping, soaring, or balancing gave me a feeling of freedom and exhileration that was addictive.

The call of the wild was always at my doorstep. The summer after high school graduation, some friends and I nearly pulled off a move to the forrest where we planned to build a cabin and live off the land.

Even as a married man with three children, I did things like walk across the top of swingsets. One experience in southern Utah finally taught me something about wisdom.

I shinnied up a 100 foot crevas between two rock walls. My dad, who should have known better, was right behind me. At the top, one wall gradually levelled off. I could see a hand hold, but I couldn't reach it. I would have to leap and hope my right hand could get a grip on it.

Throwing caution to the wind, I sprang upward and laterally at the same time. Clutching onto the hand hold, I pulled my body up. My dad, seeing that he couldn't go any further, scooted back down, and had to drive several miles around the rim to rescue me.

After this event where I risked my life in front of my wife and kids, I began drawing a line between adventure and fool hardiness.

I'm now a few years from reaching the end of my career as a registered nurse, but the thrill of high drama still burns within me. The only difference is that it now flows through the end of my pen.

If you've ever dreamed of going back in time to change your personal life or some historical event, then you have captured the essence of this book (at no actual physical danger to yourself). If the real event happened, you would do whatever was necessary in order to reach your goal. That would be a great responsibility, but it would also provide for great adventure.

Dan Busby

www.ingramcontent.com/pod-product-compliance
Lightning Source LLC
LaVergne TN
LVHW011718060526
838200LV00051B/2944